Oh, my—

My prayers had been answered. Here I was, face to face with Fun.

My pulse picked up a notch. I reminded myself, *Remember why you're here. To meet lots of weird, bad naughty people.* I would channel every ounce of annoyance and depression into Sheila Smith, and . . . Oh, who was I trying to fool? I would just end up more annoyed and depressed by faking my way through this school for the next three weeks with a rude jerk at my side. It was like a prison sentence. How would I get along with someone who spray-painted everything in sight? No matter how noble his intentions?

ALSO BY

DANIEL EHRENHAFT

Drawing a Blank

Friend Is Not a Verb

DIRTY
LAUNDRY
DANIEL EHRENHAFT

HARPER TEEN
An Imprint of HarperCollinsPublishers

HarperTeen is an imprint of HarperCollins Publishers.

 For information address HarperCollins Children's Books, a division of HarperCollins Publishers, 10 East 53rd Street, New York, NY 10022.
www.harperteen.com

Library of Congress Cataloging-in-Publication Data
Ehrenhaft, Daniel.
Dirty laundry / Daniel Ehrenhaft. — 1st ed.
p. cm.
Summary: Carli, a teen actress who has gone undercover at a New England boarding school in order to research a role, hooks up with a student graffiti artist to investigate the disappearance of another of the school's pupils.
ISBN 978-0-06-113105-9
[1. Missing persons—Fiction. 2. Boarding schools—Fiction. 3. Schools—Fiction. 4. Actors and actresses—Fiction. 5. New England—Fiction. 6. Mystery and detective stories.] I. Title.
PZ7.E3235Di 2009 2008051966
[Fic]—dc22 CIP
AC

Typography by Andrea Vandergrift
10 11 12 13 14 CG/RRDH 10 9 8 7 6 5 4 3 2 1
❖
First paperback edition, 2010

To Clare Hutton, both for editorial genius and for sticking with the *Chinese Democracy* of novels through thick and thin

Thanks to Edward Necarsulmer IV for making this happen, to Clare Hutton and Jocelyn Davies for seeing it through, and to Jess for laughs and eternal inspiration.

SHAKESPEARE'S CLOTHES SMELLED
MAYBE WORSE THAN MINE
NO DETERGENT IN ELIZABETHAN TIMES!
ALL THE WORLD WAS A STINKY STAGE
ALL THE MEN AND WOMEN FILTHY PLAYERS
WHOOPS GOTTA RUN: COPS

—Graffiti on the cliffs lining Route 16
outside Wellington, Massachusetts

WATCH OUT FOR THE LAUNDROMAT
STAINS CAN BE PERMANENT!
WE ARE NOT RESPONSIBLE FOR LOST ITEMS
SUCH AS SOCKS OR FRIENDS
SOME FREE ADVICE FOR YOU
CUZ I'M FUN AND I LOVE CHARITY

—Newer and more skillfully rendered
graffiti on the same cliffs

PART ONE

1. Draft of Headmaster Ezra Stanton's official statement regarding the disappearance of Darcy Novak from the Winchester School of the Arts, as discovered later

2. Opening comments from F. Udall Newport and Carli Gemz regarding the convoluted set of circumstances that made dealing with Darcy Novak's disappearance much more complicated than necessary

3. Transcript of the Q & A between Ezra Stanton, WWWW News, and the local authorities (edited by student Sarah Ryder for clarity) regarding Darcy Novak's disappearance

1

Draft of Headmaster Ezra Stanton's official statement regarding the disappearance of Darcy Novak from the Winchester School of the Arts, as discovered later

Good morning. As all of you know, I am Ezra Stanton, headmaster of the Winchester School of the Arts. I assume you also know why we've gathered in the quad this morning, and why the local authorities are present.

For eight months of the year, our beautiful campus, this oasis of creativity perched on the rugged coast of Massachusetts, is our shared home. [*Pause for a sentimental breath*] In a sense, we become family. A disruption of that family life affects us all. So I'd like to make a few remarks about the events that took place yesterday. After that, I'll add some thoughts. I'd prefer not to speculate. My remarks will concern what I know. My thoughts, however, will concern the institution I've proudly and humbly served for over twenty years. [*Somber audience eye contact*]

I'd also like to mention that these proceedings are being broadcast by our own student-run radio station, WWWW. While I initially objected, and still have some reservations, I laud WWWW's commitment to openness and transparency. Together, we stand united in concern for one of our own.

I implore anyone listening to help if you have any pertinent information.

Darcy Novak, a senior of ours, is missing. Darcy is the only child of Dr. Mitchell and Judy Novak of Westport, Connecticut. She is seventeen, five feet seven inches tall, and one hundred thirty pounds. Her hair is long and naturally blond; her eyes, blue. The Novaks asked me to mention that Darcy is a brilliant actress, and that she has a lovely singing voice. I think all of us who know her would vouch personally for that description.

[*Sad sigh*] As head counselor for Bishop House, a seniors-only girls' dormitory, Darcy is responsible for ensuring that her housemates are in their rooms and accounted for by ten P.M. She has never been anything but reliable. Her outstanding academic record, her commitment to Winchester, her genuine love of others—as well as impersonating others, myself included [*melancholy laugh*]—has made her a natural leader. When she requested the privilege to serve as Bishop House head counselor last year, she was unanimously confirmed. So when Darcy wasn't present to check in her dorm-mates on the first official night of school, alarm bells sounded.

For the record: Darcy Novak was last seen by a fellow student, Hilton James, at approximately three P.M. yesterday. According to Hilton, she was en route to the school's laundry facility. Hilton confessed to me late last night that he and Darcy had an argument. I've since learned that he and Darcy had an intimate relationship last spring.

Now for my thoughts: I'm aware Winchester has its critics. I could address the unfortunate moniker that has been snobbishly foisted upon us: that we're the "laundromat" of preparatory schools, that we're the last refuge for cast-offs, troublemakers, and miscreants . . . how high society's dirty laundry somehow always finds its way to our doorstep. I could even address the bitter irony of this bad joke with regard to the present situation. [*Long pause*] I won't. Darcy deserves better.

I'm not here to talk reputation or controversy. Nor am I here to shill, fund-raise, or burnish the school's image.

I'm here for Darcy Novak.

Thank you for your attention. I'm happy to take a few questions now.

2

Opening comments from Carli Gemz and F. Udall Newport regarding the convoluted set of circumstances that made dealing with Darcy Novak's disappearance much more complicated than necessary

Carli

Now, before we dive into the whole Darcy Novak insanity, I think it's important to explain how I met Fellini "Fun" Udall Newport in the first place.

Fun doesn't think so. Of course he doesn't. Fun is a contrarian. (Is that a word? I'll have to ask him.) But he agreed to go along. Actually, I think he's still embarrassed about how and why we met. Totally understandable. I'm embarrassed too. Plus, it's sort of tricky to explain, trickier than you might think.

I think it's best to start with the first time I ever *spoke* to him, the night before I left LA for Winchester. He called me.

Looking back, the call was a brave move on his part—and

completely unexpected, considering the relationship we were supposed to have, thanks to his father. At the time, I was festering in my own anxiety. There I stood, Alice at the precipice of the Rabbit Hole . . . a fledgling actress, a few weeks past my seventeenth birthday. I was about to start a new school, a new life (a fake life, true) with very little idea of what I was getting myself into. I would be leaving behind my therapist, my friends, and my personal assistant; I'd never been anywhere on the East Coast other than New York . . . and I was about to entrust all these secrets and my new identity to the stranger on the phone.

Forget anxious; I was scared.

Then Fun opened his mouth.

I'll spare you the details of the conversation. Fun can handle the details; he's better at that. Let's just say that it was short and mean and pretty humiliating. But who can blame him? When I put myself in Fun's shoes, I can't even imagine how I'd act. He had no control over the situation. He was being forced to live a lie.

Of course, I would be living a lie too. The difference was that I was getting paid to live it. It was my golden opportunity, my big chance—reality and fantasy all tied up in a freakish little bow. Fun was just along for my ride.

FUN

Oh, right: the first time I met Carli Gemz (pronounced "games"). Or the first time I spoke to her, anyway. I did indeed call her in LA the night before she flew east and moved into Bishop House.

And what, you may ask, is this fabulous-sounding Bishop House? What is this *oasis,* this *home,* whose very name evokes both sanctity and asylum? Not the insane kind of asylum, although the dorm *is* a notorious looney bin . . . *sanctuary* is the word I'm looking for. Yes: *sanctity and sanctuary*. That has a pleasant alliterative ring.

Bishop House is the crappiest dorm at Winchester, which is easily the crappiest school in New England, the crappiest part of the crappiest country in the world. It is also where Stanton consistently chooses to warehouse Winchester's supposed brightest senior girls (or, in Carli's case, girls pretending to be bright girls). Bishop House's plumbing hasn't functioned properly since the Eisenhower Administration. But who cares? The *name* sounds great. That's what matters. Looks! Surface! Everything America and Winchester stand for! U-S-A! U-S-A!

Too bad I'm still too young to vote. I will vote, though. You better freaking believe it, you gips. I mean pigs. Sorry, just channeling Nails, a.k.a. Hilton James, my best friend. God bless that kid, his leftist ideology, and his speech impediment.

I'm off topic again—my apologies. It's the ADHD. We'll get to Nails later.

Anyway, I called Carli to see what kind of a person she was. Dad showed me her head shot, so I was curious. Was she as goofy as she looked? What was up with those pigtails? Was she a spoiled brat? Did she honestly believe that wearing an undersized baby-T emblazoned with the word GIVE in pink letters (strategically positioned over her boobs) would convince me she *wasn't* one of "them"? By *them*, I mean the breed of gorgeous teen actress—as popularized on TV—who giggles through adolescence until Britney's next meltdown. It's not a cliché. These girls do in fact exist, and in droves.

Most of all, I wondered, Would Carli *fit in* at Winchester?

Well, no, obviously. It's impossible to fit in here. Even Stanton accepts this. He cops to it every year at graduation with the same moronic tripe. Which reminds me, you should have heard Darcy Novak imitate the guy. Nobody could do Stanton like she could. The very last time I saw her, in fact—the night before summer break—she snuck into our room to say good-bye and ended up giving a command performance. (I'm still not sure what prompted the surprise visit. Maybe she felt guilty about dumping Nails?) She delivered Stanton's speech to the graduating class verbatim in that high-pitched Muppet voice of his:

> *Consider our history. The school was founded in 1777 by a fiercely independent patriot, Horace Winchester. He supplied Minutemen with much-needed homemade wine to sustain them through cold nights of fighting the British. And yet because Horace Winchester was a lifelong bachelor and nude portrait painter—and because he laid the campus's foundation on his vineyard—we suffer an undeserved reputation for being a problem school with a thirst for intoxication.*

Welch's grape soda came out my nose. Nails nearly had a seizure. Horace Winchester was *gay*, Stanton—as gay as Oscar Wilde,

Larry Craig, or Elton John. He was a drunkard, too. You don't have to apologize. Celebrate it!

> *I've heard the gossip, as have you. We are Winchester: where to go if you've been caught selling dope at a real prep school, where to go if you've flunked algebra but can steal the best turntables. We're nothing more than a bunch of delinquents, cooped up in over a ramshackle hundred acres. "Even your crummy football field is pockmarked with rabbit holes!" they tell us. Well. Winchester may never boast a great football team. Our last winning season was in 1944. But we have spawned numerous giants of the entertainment industry: four Oscar nominees, a National Book Award finalist, and a Guggenheim fellow. We spawn iconoclasts, not sheep. Don't ever forget that. Live!*

Bravo, Darcy. Bravo.

Ah, Stanton, all I can do is laugh again for her sake: Ha! (Interesting: *Ah* and *ha* are the same words, reversed, like *Live!* and *evil*. Maybe Stanton has been trying to send us hidden messages.) Personally, my favorite part of the speech is always toward the end—when his eyes inevitably grow misty—about how it's our duty to "set a moral example" for those who follow us. Question: If we're so moral, how *did* we earn our reputation as the laundromat of boarding schools?

No need to answer. And Darcy didn't bother to finish. Sadly, she missed the two salient points Stanton never fails to make in conclusion:

- After graduating, we'll owe it to ourselves to donate generously to Winchester.
- If, by some miracle, some of us do attain a measure of respectability as adults, we will prove the elite wrong. And on that glorious day, Stanton will be vindicated, the chip on his shoulder will vaporize, and Winchester will join the prestigious ranks of say . . . Exeter. (Or at least South Kent.) It will only take one of us!

Oh my God, Stanton! Could it be ME? Really? Stop! You're making me blush!

Come to think of it, I'm pretty sure he plagiarized a lot of that speech. In two hundred plus years, we haven't produced any respectable alumni. Still, we've managed to squeeze out some kick-ass plagiarists. Actresses, too!

Carli

Okay, before we go any further, I should explain a few things.

I wasn't *really* going to be a Winchester student my senior year. I mean, I was, but I was going to attend in character.

A month earlier, in LA, I'd been cast for a TV pilot, *Private Nights.* (It's slated to turn from a pilot into an actual prime-time series once the network decides on a time slot.) My agent, Ingrid Botz, calls it "*Gossip Girl* meets *The Facts of Life*, but edgier!" She grabbed my chin the first time she told me this, cooing as if I were a toddler. She does that a lot. Translation if you don't speak Hollywood-ese: It's about a bunch of naughty rich girls at a swanky all-girls boarding school. It "pushes boundaries" and is "meant to provoke." (Ingrid's words again.) This means it's rated TV-M. I might be in a few scenes wearing only lingerie, and there's a hint of some same-sex intimacy. I'm supposed to kiss my roommate on the lips at some point—I think during a game of truth or dare. That could change, though. I've only read the first draft of the first script.

By the way, if you haven't seen or heard of *The Facts of Life*, I'm not surprised at all. Not a lot of people my age have. It's pretty corny. But I love it. I'm sort of a corny TV and movie addict in general.

I am a dork.

Which brings me back to the series: My character is *not* a dork. Her name is Sheila Smith, by far the worst of the bunch: the schemer who won't let anyone stand in her way, the queen bee, the foul seductress . . . place every standard Mean Girl stereotype here and then triple it. (Yikes!) But the problem is . . .

I am a dork.

All right, in some ways, I am like Sheila Smith. Of course I scheme. Of course I'm selfish. My parents always tell me to "count my blessings," but I can't count that high, and I'm not bragging, either. I've been a child actress since I was six. Mom and Dad are both rich *and* happily married. Worse, I don't need their money. Last year, I made over $200,000 after taxes. Ready to puke yet? I feel like puking, myself. But I'll stop. Dr. Fein, my therapist, calls this sort of rant a "shame spiral."

When I find myself caught in a shame spiral, Dr. Fein says

I'm supposed to do something active to get out of my own head. Like on my sixteenth birthday. Mom and Dad gave me a fully equipped BMW X5. Of course they did. But instead of beating myself up, I didn't say a word. I pasted a smile on my face and drove my brand-new car to South Central, where I'd once passed a soup kitchen on the way to a shoot: FRANNY'S FREE-4-ALL. I marched right in and volunteered. I kept it up all year, too, even after the car got stolen. Every Sunday, without fail, I ladled out steaming bowls of freeze-dried tomato or chicken broth to all in need. It felt great. Take that, shame!

The best part? The very first person I served ended up becoming my personal assistant. His name is Grizz. He's fifty-five and used to be a roadie for Kiss. How cool is that? He's been all over the world ("I got a beef on every continent"); he's covered in scars and tattoos—but he's really just a big, stinky teddy bear. He gets things done, too. He's an ace at taking my calls; they never last. Now if only he'd shave his beard and bathe regularly, other people would see him for the sweetheart he is. Dr. Fein is a genius.

FUN

We'll get to the phone call in a moment. But here's an interesting detail about Darcy Novak: To the best of my knowledge, she and Charity Barker were the only two girls in our class who never received any professional psychiatric care.

Not even a consultation. I've researched this. Every other female senior—all thirty-eight—admits to seeing a therapist regularly, or has undergone counseling. Several have been institutionalized. Yet Darcy and Charity somehow avoided shrinkage. And now they are both gone (coincidence?): Charity, because she was EXPELLED FOR NO GOOD REASON, and Darcy, because . . . well, that's the big question, isn't it?

Incidentally, Charity Barker is my girlfriend. Or she was, until she was KICKED OUT FOR SNEAKING INTO MY ROOM. A COMMON OFFENSE! SOMETHING EVERYONE IN A RELATIONSHIP DOES! WE DIDN'T EVEN HAVE SEX! WHY DID YOU DO IT, STANTON? WHY DID YOU KICK HER OUT, YOU JACKASS?

I'll lose the caps. I'm not trying to make a statement. I don't go for melodrama, like, "Watch out, I'm an angry young man!" I'm just being honest. I'm not a filthy player, like the graffiti says. All the world is not a stage. Not for me, anyway.

On the other hand, even if Charity were still around, I do have the right to be a tad angry. Start with my name: Fellini. My father named me in honor of his idol. And no, I haven't seen *La Vida Loca*, or whatever it's called, or any other of Fellini's crappy movies. (Actually, it's called *La Dolce Vita* and I *have* seen it. That was meant to piss Dad off.) If you think having a name like Fellini is cool or hip or avant garde, pretend you're a five-year-old boy. Think of the words that rhyme with Fellini: *teeny*, *weeny*, the unprintable, et cetera. Now picture a school yard teeming with fat bullies.

But this prenatal assignation wasn't my father's most egregious misdeed. Nor was telling me that graffiti was a "gangster's pastime." (His real words!) Nor was confiscating my paint cans, grounding me a dozen times, or shipping me off to Winchester because I wrote my name all over LA in ten-foot-high letters.

No, the most egregious misdeed, by far, was forcing me to be an "actress's assistant" in order to graduate. I have to give him credit. He is the world's ballsiest liar. I'll never forget what he told me that night I first called Carli Gemz, lounging in our sumptuous dining room as he gazed at me over a pungent heap of Chinese takeout . . . It was beautiful. "You won't be doing me a service, son," he said. "You won't be doing Carli Gemz a service, either. You'll be doing *yourself* a service."

I almost laughed. Wow. Maybe I *could* become respectable, just like Stanton said! Dad was right. My future depended on getting my hands on that pesky, elusive Winchester diploma, and Carli Gemz was my only ticket. I needed her. And sure, Dad may have needed her for his ingenious new "teensploitation" TV show, *Private Nights*. But I would be benefiting the most. What a lie to believe in!

Carli

Jonathan Newport understood that I was a dork, and that I needed to "de-dork." To this day, I believe that this is what sparked his crazy plan—this and the fact that he was desperate for his son to complete high school. So it made sense, in a totally unorthodox way: While *Private Nights* awaited final word on its scheduling, I would spend a few weeks "undercover" at his son's boarding school. I would go as Sheila Smith. I would rehearse *being* her, every single waking moment. I would soak up the "bona fides" (his term) of a real-life prep school. And once the project was officially given the green light, I'd vanish, readier than ever to tackle the role. He'd work out the logistics. What did I think?

Conundrum!

Well, several conundra, ethically speaking . . . but one particularly big one. I needed a personal assistant in order to sign on. It's a standard clause in all my contracts. (Ingrid's call, not mine.) Needless to say, Grizz made going to an East Coast prep school in character impossible. He couldn't exactly pose as a fellow student or roommate. I doubt he'd even pass as a janitor. Not at a boarding school.

"No worries!" Jonathan Newport exclaimed. "You can use my son!"

I can still hear him marveling at his own genius.

Were it not for this peculiar confluence of events, I would have had to refuse the role. Which means Fellini "Fun" Udall Newport would have been expelled. Which means as far as Darcy Novak goes . . . Well, like Headmaster Stanton said, there's no point in speculating. All the pieces were in place. Somehow, with the wave of a magic wand (i.e., a massive sum of money, plus some other perks), Jonathan Newport sold Headmaster Stanton on the idea. Fun would graduate, so long as he helped me out. I would attend Winchester for as long as needed—probably no longer than a few weeks—as Sheila Smith. Nobody except Headmaster Stanton and Fun would know my true identity.

It was beyond weird. It was fake life becoming real life, only to become fake (and real) again. It *was* Alice and the Rabbit Hole.

Oh, and one last little aside: The day I signed the contract, Headmaster Stanton sent me an e-mail assuring me that my secret identity would be safe. He joked that he'd "already formed an image of Sheila Smith's character" and that he'd watch out for me. He also enclosed JPEGs of Fun's graffiti to help me form an image of the young man who would be my new assistant—adding that, in spite of the vandalism, I shouldn't be nervous. That at heart, Fun was a decent kid. His past offenses had been forgiven.

The pictures were pretty much all the same. Well, not exactly. Some were more intricate, some were hastily scrawled, some were colorful, others monochromatic, but the words never changed: "I'm Fun And I Love Charity."

That cracked me up. They *did* help me form an image of Fun, exactly like Headmaster Stanton said. He broke the rules, yes. But deep down he liked to do positive things for people. He just boasted about it in the wrong way.

FUN

I know, the phone call, already. No preamble this time. The conversation speaks for itself on a variety of levels. Plus it has been burned into my memory for all eternity, and even without the ensuing Darcy Novak drama, I'm sure I would have remembered it word for word, ADHD or not.

CARLI: Hello? Jonathan? Is that you? Thanks so much for—

ME: It's not Jonathan.

CARLI: Uh . . . sorry. Who's this?

ME: Fun.

CARLI: The caller ID says—

ME: I'm Fun. Grizz's replacement.

CARLI: Oh, hi! You're Jonathan Newport's *son*!

ME: Right, your slave. I was wondering if you had any questions about Winchester. You do know that we're the laundromat of boarding schools, right?

CARLI: Excuse me?

ME: Never mind. Do you have any questions?

CARLI: Are you okay?

ME: Don't worry about me. I'm at your service. I'm at *my* service.

CARLI: What?

ME: Ask me something about Winchester.

CARLI: Well . . . I don't know . . . I mean, I've been e-mailing the headmaster, and he sent me a bunch of materials, like the bulletin and everything, and they gave me my own school e-mail address . . . The campus looks so pretty! Especially my dorm! And I'm really excited for the classes! Will the leaves start to turn while I'm there?

ME: For Christ's sake.

CARLI: Huh?

ME: I'm calling to see if you have any *real* questions. Ask me something normal. Like, "Where can I score some vodka?" Or, "Can I cheat off your homework?" Or, "What's the largest amount of nitrous oxide I can inhale safely in one sitting?"

CARLI: That's normal?

ME: For Sheila Smith, yes. I read the first draft of the first script.

CARLI: Yeah, I mean . . . it's just . . . I'm not Sheila Smith, though.

ME: Wrong. You *are* Sheila Smith. And even if Sheila Smith is a slut with no morals, she's articulate.

CARLI: Sure, I guess . . . but I mean—

ME: Stop stammering, Sheila.

CARLI: Sorry. Well. As far as the bad stuff goes, I'd rather not participate, you know? I'm just there to watch and hang out, to soak it up rather than engage in it. So, actually, I do have a question. Is there something I can get involved with outside of school, on the side? Like, does the town have a favorite local charity or something?

ME: I had a favorite local Charity.

CARLI: You do?

ME: I used to. Now I don't.

CARLI: What was it? Did you volunteer somewhere?

ME: I vandalized school property with spray paint.

CARLI: Oh . . . yeah. Headmaster Stanton sent me some JPEGs of your graffiti. But he said he forgave you! That was nice of him.

ME: If you say so.

CARLI: Well, it's cool that he has a spirit of forgiveness or whatever . . . That's what I love about the

Winchester Bulletin, too. The stuff he wrote at the end about it's the duty of the graduating class to set a "moral example"—

ME: Stanton didn't forgive anything, you ditz. My dad bribed him to keep me in school. That's why I'm your slave.

CARLI: Oh.

ME: Charity is my girlfriend.

CARLI: Girlfriend?

ME: Charity Barker. She was my muse.

CARLI: I'm sorry. I'm really confused.

ME: I'll spell it out for you, Sheila. I tagged most of the campus with Charity's name, inflicting hundreds of dollars' worth of damage. But I was never caught in the act. Charity didn't have the same luck. Stanton himself caught her trying to sneak into my dorm room. She cost the school nothing. But somehow, she got booted and I didn't, because my dad made a Faustian bargain with him. Get it now?

CARLI: Um . . . a *what* bargain?

ME: Faustian. Evil! A pact with—Oh, forget it. I'll see you tomorrow. In case you don't know what I look like, I'm the short, pissed-off-looking blond guy who sold his soul to Satan for a diploma. I mean Stanton. Same difference.

(*Click*)

Understand how the conversation speaks for itself? You think a word (for instance, *charity*) means one thing, but it really means another. Just like you think a head shot means one thing and it doesn't. Or a single phone conversation, for that matter.

Carli

There is a punch line to all this. Hee, hee . . .

The part I left out, and that I didn't tell Fun for a long, long time—even post Darcy Novak—is that I *know* Charity Barker. I mean, I know who she is. Actually, screw it—after everything that's happened, I've come to realize that this is a really stupid and silly thing to say about someone: *"I know who she is."* How could I know anything about her? I only met her once, at an audition for an independent movie that was supposed to star Rip Torn. (I don't think it ever got made.)

What I *can* say, however, is that Charity Barker did not make a great first impression. Normally actresses smile and make polite chit-chat in the waiting room. We know we're competing for the same part, but there's a sort of camaraderie, an unspoken "we're-all-in-it-together" vibe. We wish one another good luck, and we mean it.

Not Charity. She sat there, avoiding eye contact, chewing Orbit and reading *Vogue*. She even took a cell-phone call—definitely a no-no in audition waiting-room etiquette—and cackled as if nobody else was around.

As fate would have it, we were assigned to read a scene together.

Charity was terrible. Bad acting feeds on itself, so she made *me* terrible. She accidentally kept reading my lines instead of hers.

She giggled a lot and never apologized once. She didn't even shake my hand or say good-bye when it was over. She just popped a fresh piece of Orbit into her mouth, clicked on her phone, and marched out into the sunshine to keep yammering.

Not exactly professional.

But for all I know, she might have had a lousy day. Maybe she was caught in a shame spiral. Maybe she'd decided to play up the "not-so-bright alternative chick" for the audition. Maybe the whole performance was an act, even the waiting-room stuff. Maybe afterward—safely out of eyesight and earshot—she went somewhere to read stories to blind children, and didn't flub a single word.

I guess this is just a long way of saying that if I'd decided at the last minute to forego Jonathan Newport's plan and stay in LA—if that phone call had completely turned me off on the whole idea (and it almost did)—I might think differently about Fun, too.

I might not think about him at all.

Then, who knows what would have happened to Darcy Novak?

3

Transcript of the Q & A between Ezra Stanton, WWWW News, and the local authorities (edited by student Sarah Ryder for clarity), regarding Darcy Novak's disappearance

WWWW NEWS: Stanton, regarding yesterday . . .

EZRA STANTON: *Headmaster* Stanton, Sarah.

WWWW NEWS: Sorry, Headmaster Stanton. You stated that our schoolmate, Hilton James, had an intimate relationship with the missing senior?

WELLINGTON POLICE LIEUTENANT GEORGE JACOBS: We're not discussing any potential suspects right now.

WWWW NEWS: Sorry, officer? You're saying Hilton James is a potential suspect?

EZRA STANTON: No, Sarah, he didn't say that. The question was addressed to me. And I didn't say that, either. I have absolutely no idea what happened to Darcy.

WELLINGTON POLICE LIEUTENANT
GEORGE JACOBS: Correct. So the answer still stands: We're not discussing any potential suspects right now.

WWWW NEWS: Well, let me try a different angle. To your knowledge, Headmaster Stanton, has Darcy Novak had intimate relations with any student besides Hilton James?

EZRA STANTON: Sarah, don't be coy. Everyone here knows Darcy and Kirk Bishop became close at the end of last semester. But there is no possible way Kirk could—

WELLINGTON POLICE LIEUTENANT
GEORGE JACOBS: I think we have time for one more question, and then we should wrap this up. We've got work to do.

WWWW NEWS: Headmaster Stanton? You mentioned Kirk Bishop? Is he a suspect?

EZRA STANTON: Enough, Sarah. No. Of course not. Kirk Bishop's family has been a part of the Winchester community for five generations. Bishop House, the very dorm where Darcy is a head counselor, bears—

WELLINGTON POLICE LIEUTENANT
GEORGE JACOBS: Staton, Idon't mean to be short, but it's best to keep quiet.

EZRA STANTON: It's Headmaster Stanton.

WELLINGTON POLICE LIEUTENANT
GEORGE JACOBS: Excuse me?

EZRA STANTON: I prefer to be called Headmaster Stanton.

WELLINGTON POLICE LIEUTENANT
GEORGE JACOBS: Thankyouagainforyourtime,everyone. Good-bye.

EZRA STANTON: What's with the attitude?

WELLINGTON POLICE LIEUTENANT
GEORGE JACOBS: What?

EZRA STANTON: I know you applied here several years ago. You were denied admission. I'm sorry. But please, let it go. It wasn't personal. You didn't have the grades.

WELLINGTON POLICE LIEUTENANT
GEORGE JACOBS: What are you. . . ? My mom made me apply! You think I wanted to go to this dump? You've been bringing in a bunch of drugged-out homos to do God-knows-what for hundreds of years!

EZRA STANTON: Please stop. I'll file a complaint with the chief of police. This isn't about you or your mom or "homos," or even the school. It's about Darcy Novak.

WELLINGTON POLICE LIEUTENANT
GEORGE JACOBS: Who *disappeared* from the school, right? Like I said, it is a dump. You know it; everyone knows it. It's falling apart. You're going bankrupt. Think this girl would have disappeared from Hotchkiss? Go ahead. File a complaint with the chief. He'll get a good laugh.

WWWW NEWS: I'm sorry, Lieutenant Jacobs? The school is going bankrupt?

EZRA STANTON: No, Sarah. He didn't mean . . . Give me that microphone—

(End transmission)

PART TWO

1 Fun tries to console Nails while avoiding the dreaded issue of Carli. Meanwhile, Carli adopts her false "Sheila Smith" identity for the very first time.

2 Fun and Carli meet. Headmaster Stanton instructs students not to do their own laundry but to send it out to the new "private cleaning service," as the police have cordoned off the area surrounding the school's laundromat.

3 Carli meets some of the more dubious members of the Winchester faculty and student body. Later, Fun and Carli share a few ambiguous moments.

4 Fun notices something odd about Nails's speech; Carli has three unfortunate exchanges; talk turns to action.

5 Taking action comes at a price.

1

Fun tries to console Nails while avoiding the dreaded issue of Carli. Meanwhile, Carli adopts her false "Sheila Smith" identity for the very first time.

FUN

"Stop worrying, Nails."

I'd repeated these three words exactly thirteen times in the past ten minutes. They weren't having the soothing effect I'd hoped. Nails continued to pace our room, running his fingers through his spiky black hair. I wanted to grab him and shout at him the way that Wellington cop had just shouted at Stanton. *Relax! Let's talk about normal stuff. Like how every fall you try to look like more of a washed-up Brit-pop failure. Who are you trying to be right now? You don't even play an instrument!* Since June, his waistline had shrunk and his skin had whitened. How anyone could return from a carefree, jobless summer as bone thin and corpse pale as Nails was yet another unsolved mystery of the morning. His ratty "James Brown Sex Machine" T-shirt didn't help matters.

"Ten to one this is some kind of gag, Nails. Don't listen to what Stanton said on the radio. You should listen to the cop. You're not a suspect. There are no suspects. Maybe Darcy is just taking a very long nap somewhere."

He stopped pacing. "I know you're trying to be funny. You always try to impress me when you haven't seen me in a while."

"Busted. That's me, the Nutty Comedian out to impress the Funky Albino."

Nails sighed. He flopped down on the unmade bed that would theoretically be his for the year—unless he was arrested or expelled, or both. "I don't care about that cop, and I don't care about Stanton," he grumbled. "I care about *her*."

"Well, like I said, I'm sure there's some kind of reasonable explanation," I said. I should probably have kept my mouth shut. I was sounding like my dad.

I glanced at the boxes between us. All we'd unpacked so far was Nails's stereo, in keeping with our tradition of cranking bootlegged hip-hop and fighting over whose arcane tastes were superior. (Mine.) But first we always tuned into WWWW, Winchester's beloved 10-watt radio station—broadcast range: maybe one thousand yards. Our plan was to bask in the frothing bombast of DJ Sarah Ryder, the Death Metal Queen, who'd somehow seized control of the airwaves since freshman year (did she even attend classes?) and who always welcomed students "Back to hell!" with the same obscure German industrial cover of Pat Benatar's *Hell Is for Children*.

Instead, there was no music. We sat stupefied as Sarah transformed herself into a Geraldo-style investigative journalist. What *happened* to people over summer break?

"Sorry for the earlier interruption," she announced, her strident voice echoing across our bare walls. "Stanton is up to his usual tricks, paying lip service to the First Amendment while censoring WWWW. Hilton James, a.k.a. Nails, knows. I could go on, but I'm back in the studio, where there's been a shocking development in the Darcy Novak story. Thanks to sources who wish to remain anonymous, I've come into possession of some very sensitive audio: Stanton's interrogation of Hilton James. Judging from its content, I doubt old Nails knew the conversation was being recorded . . ."

Nails jerked up in bed. His wide eyes met mine. We stared at each other, aghast. There were a few loud clicks, followed by a hiss of static. All of a sudden Stanton's garbled voice filled the room:

> *"What were doing out by the laundry facility, Mr. James?"*
>
> *"I told you, I was taking a walk."*

I blinked. Nails remained frozen, jaw open and hands clamped over his cheeks like the emaciated ghoul in that Edvard Munch painting, *The Scream*.

> *"Taking a walk?"*
>
> *"Yeah. It was a nice day, my first day, and the campus was pretty deserted . . . I don't know. I didn't feel like hanging*

out alone in my room. Fun doesn't get here until tomorrow. I can't really unpack until he gets here with his stuff."

"And you just happened to walk out by the laundry facility."

"Yes! Listen, why are you hassling me? You should really be talking to Kirk. He's Darcy's boyfriend. And why aren't you out looking for her? It's past midnight!"

"We are *looking for her. I've notified the police. We're doing all we can. In the meantime, I'd like to get back to this argument you two had."*

"It wasn't an argument. I told you, I was teasing her."

"About what?"

"About doing her laundry! She had this huge sack of clothes with her. Classes haven't even started. And sure, she's a fashion victim, but there was no way even Darcy Novak could have run through that many clothes in such a short time. Don't you get it?"

"Get what, Mr. James?"

"She brought the bag as a prop in case she ran into you or some other member of the faculty. She's smart. She was headed somewhere else to do something . . . you know, un-Darcy. She isn't the saint you think she is. But like I said, talk to Kirk."

"Kirk Bishop is not your concern."

There was another click. Sarah chuckled. "What follows is slightly more graphic in content. I'd play it, but even WWWW has to comply with the FCC."

Nails's lips twisted. He hopped out of bed and snapped off the radio.

"Jesus! I don't believe this. How did Sarah Ryder get her hands on that? You know, I bet Stanton gave it to her himself. Seriously. You wanna bet what happened? Darcy had some freak accident and died. I bet a rotted tree fell on her, and the school is liable, so Stanton got rid of the body and is trying to pin it on me. That way he won't have to pay the settlement. You heard what the cop said. The school is bankrupt—"

"Nails, shh," I whispered. "Listen to yourself. You're starting to sound like an actual insane person, not just a disturbed young man who plays one at school."

He scowled.

"Darcy will turn up," I reassured him. "You know what *I* bet? She had a meltdown. Think about it. She's never seen a shrink, not once in her life. And who here doesn't see a shrink? It should be a requirement. It's senior year. Think of the stress: being a dorm counselor; college applications; the fall musical, which is *Grease*, so there's all this added pressure to measure up to the movie version—"

"Please fut up, Shun," he interrupted.

"Shine, I'll fut up."

At long last I caught a glimpse of his old smirk. "I thought you wouldn't poke fun at my peach insteadiment," he muttered.

"But I love peaches."

He slumped back down on the mattress. "Darcy doesn't melt down. I'm not kidding. The more pressure, the cooler she is.

Remember last spring when Stanton interrogated *her*? You know, about that A-plus she got on that essay I wrote for her about how epistemology is flawed?"

"What's epistemology again?"

"The theory of knowledge. He knew that I wrote it. And she knew he knew."

"Yeah, but if epistemology is flawed, your essay proved that neither of them knows anything," I joked lamely.

He shot me a withering glare. "Fun, you're not funny. We've been over this. *I'm* funny. Which is the whole freaking point: Stanton knows that only someone as wickedly quitty could raft such a—I mean, as wickedly witty could craft such a brilliant essay."

I shook my head. "What does that have to do with Darcy?"

"It's proof of a prior bad act. Stanton has something on me. In his eyes, I'm already a criminal. Think about it. I'm the perfect patsy. I'm better than Oswald. And the only crime I ever committed was trying to help my girlfriend, who wound up dumping me for a *real* crook. The irony!"

"Well . . ." I bit my lip.

His eyes hardened. "Well what?"

"Not to nitpick, but crime-wise, you also wrote that special request for the Book Society. Remember?" I chewed a fingernail. "About how they should be allowed to meet in a private room in the library? You finagled two hundred bucks out of Kirk Bishop to write it for him, and then you signed his name."

Nails let out a bitter little laugh. "Glad you remembered."

I sighed. "Nails—"

"Go ahead. Testify against me."

"Jesus, Nails, what I'm saying is, if anyone would want to set you up, it's Kirk Bishop! Think about it: He'd have something to gain if you got kicked out."

"Like what? He already stole my girlfriend."

"Right, which means on some level he's jealous of you. You dated her first. And since you were partners in crime, you're somebody who can incriminate *him*. Only you and he—and me, I guess—know you used the two hundred bucks he paid you to buy an illicit coffee machine." I pointed at a battered, duct-taped International Gourmet Coffeemaker box sloppily marked KEEP HIDDEN, sitting next to a smaller, plain box marked LIFTERS. "You meant *filters*, right? Not that I'm poking fun at your disability right now, Nails. I swear. I dig the coffee machine. The coffee in the dining hall sucks."

Nails almost smiled. "Maybe I did mean lifters." His puffy eyes glittered sadly. "Like those old Coca-Cola ads, the ones we learned about in History of Advertising? When Coke had cocaine in it? Remember how Darcy made me take that class? Of course you do. You never forget anything. 'Coca-Cola: Will Give You a Lift!'"

"Nails, I'm—"

"Speaking of crime, how did *you* manage to come back here, Fun? Weren't you supposed to be expelled with Charity?"

Yes, Nails. Yes, I was. But I can't tell you how or why I saved myself. It's not because I'm afraid of violating the Faustian pact I made with my Dad and Stanton . . . it's that I'm simply too embarrassed I made the deal at all. You wouldn't believe me if I told you.

"Hey, I don't mind that you're back," he added in the silence. His gaze fell to the floor. "But you gotta admit, this room would make a sweet single, especially for crime."

Carli

So, I walked into my dorm room for the first time, and—

A girl I'd never seen before was sitting alone, crying.

I'd been at Winchester less than an hour. In a way, I suppose I should have been relieved. Normally, consoling a perfect stranger in the midst of a full-fledged breakdown is a great way to snap out of a shame spiral. But after the events of the morning . . . after a massive limo had picked me up at the airport, a limo that had been surreptitiously hired by my boss, the boss whose son was supposed to be my new secret assistant . . . I felt nauseated. Staring at this sobbing girl, all I could think was, *I can't even tell her my own name.* (In my mind, I was already on Dr. Fein's couch.) *This is a nightmare.*

I cleared my throat. "Hello?"

The girl glanced up at me from her bed.

"I'm sorry," she said, wiping her eyes. "I'm Miranda. Miranda Jenkins."

"You don't have to apologize," I murmured. "I'm Car—I'm carsick."

"Pardon?"

I laughed, much too loudly. "It was a long trip from the airport! I flew in from LA and the closest airport is Boston. Er,

Logan. That's a couple of hours away. I'm just a little queasy. My name is Sheila Smith. It's nice to meet you."

She tried to smile through her tears. I dropped my bags in the doorway.

The room was a lot smaller than I had expected. A lot dustier, too. From the outside, Bishop House looked like a gingerbread mansion, something out of *Leave it to Beaver*: wide porch, white wood paneling, gorgeous clapboard shutters. They'd even included a photo of it on the cover of the most recent *Winchester Bulletin.* But on the inside . . . with the scuffed floors and cracked paint and the dueling Ikea desk/bed/chair units (one with a bare mattress), it bore a frightening resemblance to the back room at Franny's Free-4-All, where Grizz liked to catch a quick catnap after soup. This poor girl! I'd sob too if I were a new senior like me. I mean, a real new senior. We'd *both* been fooled.

"I'm not like this all the time, I swear. I just—" Miranda blew her nose into a Kleenex, and then paused. "Wow, you're pretty. I love your pigtails."

"Uh, thanks." I wasn't quite sure how to respond. "I love your hair too."

I wasn't just being nice; it was true. She'd done it in an old-fashioned blond bob that perfectly framed her round face and olive eyes. Now that I thought about it, she had a sort of yard-sale-locket vibe: the fading rosy portrait of a grandma as a hot teenager. And her outfit was great—a white thermal undershirt and denim overalls, like the kind I'd worn in seventh grade. A friendship bracelet dangled from her wrist. Childlike but not childish. I almost wanted to hug her.

"Hey, do you need a few minutes alone?" I asked. "I can get us some coffee . . ."

"No thanks." She sniffled once more and straightened. "That's cool of you to offer. I promise I'm not crazy. Definitely not as crazy as some kids here."

I nodded anxiously. Yesterday, Jonathan Newport had briefed me on the nutcases I might be shacked up with, concluding with a frightening rapid-fire warning:

"Remember, you're only there for a few weeks, tops. Incoming seniors are always the worst freaks of the bunch. So if you're stuck with an eight-hundred-pounder who shows you her taxidermy collection right off the bat, roll with it, sweetie. And don't be surprised if your roommate is jealous of how hot you are. Sheila Smith loves that kind of thing. How did Ingrid describe you? 'Penelope Cruz meets Sandra Bullock, but soft'? Money in the bank! Your agent overcharges me, by the way. Joking! I'll pony up. I gotta take some calls now. Be in touch."

"Hey, you look familiar," Miranda said. "Were you in a Skittles commercial?"

My stomach dropped.

Yes, I was in a Skittles commercial. But that was two years ago, ancient history. These days it was only broadcast during *Seinfeld* reruns. Jonathan Newport had warned me about this, too: If anybody at Winchester identified me as, say, the daughter on *Deadbeat Dad*, a horrible canceled sit-com about a single slacker father who floated from crappy job to crappy job—"*Next week he's your pizza delivery guy!"* (Thankfully, it never went into syndication)—I should just laugh it off and say, "I get that all the time."

Dr. Fein had also warned me about this. *"I don't think you should go to Winchester at all. But if someone does recognize you, do your breathing exercises."*

I couldn't. I was frozen. The silence stretched between us.

"Are you okay?" Miranda asked.

"It's funny, people always ask me about the Skittles commercial—I get that all the time!" I exclaimed. "But, no, I'm just the spitting image of the girl who was in it, I guess. Listen, um, I should probably take a look around campus. Seeing as I'm new."

Miranda giggled.

"What?" I said.

"I'm new too. But you probably knew that. Why did *you* get sent here?"

Panic took hold. I began to hyperventilate. I could feel my face turning sushi pink. *I am doomed. This is never going to work.*

"It's just that you don't strike me as somebody who needs help," Miranda added.

"Wha–What do you mean?"

"I'm the one who's been crying," she answered wryly.

She flashed another disarming smile. Her cheeks were still wet.

Keep the conversation going, I ordered myself. I shoved my clammy palms into my pockets. I resisted the overwhelming urge to confess everything. The unspoken words bounced around my skull: *Miranda, you look like a really nice girl, and so lonely and homesick—so, you want to hear something funny? You're right. I don't need help. I was hired to come here because I'm an actress. This is a job!*

"Do you mind that I picked a bed already?" she asked. "I got here last night."

"Not at all."

"Can I ask you something, Sheila?"

"Uh . . . sure."

"Why *are* you here? Seriously. Not to pry, but everyone gets sent here for something. Winchester is where all the real sickos end up—especially new seniors. But you don't look so bad. You don't look like you've ever even gotten a zit."

"I . . ." I could feel the internal monologue starting again. *Turn it off.* The problem was she'd pegged me. I wasn't a sicko. Not even literally. I hadn't had a cold in years. And I'd only gotten one zit that I knew of—behind my ear, so you couldn't even see it. Which was why I felt guilty all the time. Which was why I volunteered at the soup kitchen. Which was why all my friends back home thought I was insane. Spiral!

And Miranda, if you want, I can make you some soup, I imagined telling her. *It's really soothing. It's comfort food. I'm a great soup chef! Cooking gets me out of my head, too. It's even one of the skills I listed on my résumé, because a lot of family movies want "older-sibling realism" in teenage female characters.*

"I'm sorry," Miranda said. "Forget it. I'm making you uncomfortable."

"No, it's cool." I steeled myself. I slouched. I was Sheila

Smith, and Sheila Smith didn't even know what a shame spiral *was*. "I wound up here because of bad grades. And partying and stuff. How about you?"

"I got caught boning my gym teacher."

What the—I was no longer Sheila Smith. "Really?" I whispered.

"Yeah, in the girls' locker room." Her smile widened. "Why? Are you offended?"

I stared down at the luggage at my feet. "No . . . I just . . . I wasn't expecting that."

"That a geek like me could land a hot teacher?"

My head jerked up. "No! I think you're really cute! I mean, not like *that*. I mean I'm straight. Oh, jeez. I should just shut up."

She giggled again. "I'm teasing. Even if you aren't straight, it's fine. This is Winchester, right? But it's not as sordid as it sounds. He was twenty-two. Also, I bet I'm older than you. I turn nineteen in December. It was just one of those spur-of-the-moment, totally inappropriate romances . . ." She sighed, sounding very old. "Okay, now *I* should shut up. Who really wants to hear a total stranger's life story?"

I shrugged. I wouldn't mind hearing it. At least Miranda's life story was real.

FUN

The moment Nails mentioned the word "crime," my thoughts turned from Darcy. It's pathetic, but my instinctive reaction was, *Carli Gemz is probably already on campus.*

Like me, she'd taken the red-eye cross-country last night. Thank God we'd flown on different airlines. It would only be hours (maybe even minutes; crap, it was already 9:30 A.M.!) before she tracked me down. And then we'd have to have an actual conversation, in person. About the BS of managing her credit-card debt or complimenting her shoes or whatever the hell else an assistant did (and I was now certain her infantile head shot reflected an infantile intellect). Sheesh. Talk about a crime.

"Maybe we should start unpacking," Nails suggested quietly. "It'll distract us."

I nodded. "Good idea. Let's start with the coffeemaker." I leaned back on the mattress and rubbed my eyes.

"Hey, Fun, can I ask you something?"

"For the last time, I am not worried about Darcy," I lied.

"It's not about Darcy. Did you hang with Charity much this summer in LA?"

"Not so much." I ignored the tightening knot in my gut. "She was busy with auditions." *Way too busy,* I added in miserable, self-pitying silence.

"So are you guys over, or what?"

"I don't think so." I couldn't tell if this falsehood was for his benefit or mine. Charity hadn't exactly been communicative. We only lived an hour apart, two hours if the traffic sucked. In theory we could have hung out every day. But something had changed. Namely: I got snubbed. She said the expulsion was a sign that she couldn't cling to the past. She also claimed she still loved me, but she was going to use the summer months to focus on auditions, to further her career. She didn't even return my last text. And apparently her hard work paid off. She was cast in a Black Eyed Peas video. Fantastic! And shouldn't we share this triumph? Wasn't I still tagging her name?

Not good enough. And on second thought, screw her.

Really, Charity, please, I said to myself. *Don't be mad at me. Sorry I wasn't expelled. But you're not a star. The ditz I'm supposed to babysit was cast in a TV pilot! Are you blowing up so huge that you can't shoot off a single lame-but-acceptable text message? Huh?* luv u fun can't talk xox, C *How hard is that? You have ONE claim to fame: a fuzzy split-second exploitative shot of your butt in a video that nobody will even remember. My father's a director; I know this stuff. I'm the one who appreciates you—*

"Fun?" Nails asked. "You all right? You're fidgeting."

I swallowed. "Yeah, I know. I just have to deal. Charity's not here, and I am."

"I hear you." Nails stood. He shuffled to the dusty panes of our lone window, staring across the muddy football field toward the gnarled vineyards at the edge of campus. In that light, he didn't look so much like a Brit-pop failure. He looked like a vagrant in need of a good night's sleep. In a sense, he was.

"So we're both single again," he mused. "Why the hell should I even care about what happened to Darcy? She dumped me for Kirk Bishop."

I nodded queasily. "Right on."

He smiled. "Besides, it's senior year. Like they say in *Grease*, or at least on the seminal TV program *Grease: You're the One That*

I Want, 'We are gonna rule the school.' "

"That was the Pink Ladies, Nails."

"Whatever. I'm okay with my sexual ambiguity." He sighed and turned to me. "But I wonder if I could find some hot new senior transfer to bang. That would really help take my mind off Darcy. You know of any hot new senior transfers, Fun?"

Carli

It took me several minutes to muster the courage to step across the threshold of my tiny new room. I nearly tripped over my bags. All I could think as I shook hands with my new roommate was, *This girl is way smarter than I am.* Miranda used the words *sordid* and *inappropriate* in casual conversation. Dr. Fein didn't even do that.

"Are you sure you don't want a moment alone?" I kept asking.

"This is your room, too, sweetie," she reassured me. "But it is a lot to deal with at once, isn't it?"

I mustered a smile. "You got that right."

"I just can't believe it. It's crazy, you know? Our dorm counselor is missing! She was supposed to check me in last night. I was the first one here, and—"

"Whoa," I cut in. "I'm sorry. What are you talking about? Who's missing?"

Miranda scrunched her eyebrows. "Our dorm counselor. Darcy Novak?" She stated the name as if I should instantly recognize it, like it was Brangelina. "You don't know? Oh my God! You didn't hear that stuff on the school radio?"

"No . . ." I shook my head. My throat was suddenly dry.

"*That's* why I was crying," Miranda said. "I mean, I know I'm brand new, but I felt like I knew her. Seriously, it was like I had a built-in friend here. She sent me an amazingly sweet e-mail this summer. 'Welcome to Winchester! I hear you like the theater, and you were in a book club. Me too! Anyway, it's hard being a senior transfer, so if you need anything, I can help, yada, yada, yada . . .' When I e-mailed back, we struck up a correspondence." Miranda hesitated. "You didn't get a welcome e-mail from Darcy?"

"No."

"I bet it got spammed," she said. "Darcy said she e-mailed everyone."

"I bet you're right," I answered automatically.

Now my character was kicking in. Oh, yes. Sheila Smith had returned. And she was legitimately pissed. Not at Miranda of course. At Jonathan Newport.

He deleted the e-mail, I thought, clenching my jaw. *He owns the name "Sheila Smith," so he owns sheilasmith@winchesterarts.edu. He's screwing with me. Probably so I'll get off on the wrong foot. He wants me to be angry and confused and insecure. He wants me to FEEL like Sheila Smith. It's one thing to method act; it's another thing to be manipulated! How can I portray someone if I don't know everything I'm supposed to know? Some girl disappeared??? A life may be in danger! A real one!*

"Listen, I didn't mean to freak you out with all this," Miranda said. "You can unpack if you want. Just let me know if you need some of my drawers or anything."

I stared at my paltry belongings: a laptop, a Louis Vuitton purse, and a Tumi bag.

The contents—mostly slinky dresses—wouldn't take up a single one of my Ikea drawers, much less any of Miranda's.

There was no way I could pull this off. I should have listened to Dr. Fein. I shouldn't have signed up for this gig. True, the salary was off the charts. I could renovate Franny's Free-4-All with it. I could build a chain of Franny's Free-4-Alls. I'd lose my mind, but I'd have a lot of money to give away. Cold comfort for hot soup. Ha! *"Don't worry, doll, we'll yank you out of Winchester if anyone gets suspicious,"* Ingrid had told me a dozen times. I knew she didn't mean it. She didn't coo. She was well aware I wouldn't arrive looking like a troubled new senior. I'd arrive looking like the phony I was. Which reminded me, I still had to find Fun. That was something active, I supposed. At least it would prevent me from wallowing in my own head.

"You don't want to unpack?" Miranda asked.

"I'll unpack later," I mumbled. "This girl who disappeared . . . Her name's Darcy?"

"Yeah." Miranda's face brightened. "Hey, what do you say we try to get the inside scoop on this whole situation? We can check out the campus for a couple of hours together, on our own. We have some time to kill. I mean, we're supposed to go to some big orientation luncheon at the dining hall, but that's it. Did you get that e-mail?"

I shook my head. "Nope. Didn't get that one, either."

"Oh, well. I think we're required to go." She arched an eyebrow. "The food is awful, but maybe we'll meet some cute guys. Let's get out of here."

I had to laugh. My dorm counselor was AWOL . . . but hey, cute guys! If Jonathan Newport's goal was to throw me off by deleting all my e-mails, I supposed he'd succeeded. I needed to channel that rage and frustration. Cute guys would help. Bring 'em on. I'd taken a step closer to becoming Sheila Smith.

"That sounds great," I told Miranda.

The funny thing? The advice both Jonathan Newport and Dr. Fein had given me, in classic devil-on-one-shoulder, angel-on-the-other style? The advice on how to make my short stint here work *without* going insane?

It was, "Tell the truth whenever you can."

For the first and possibly last time at Winchester, I just had.

2

Fun and Carli meet. Headmaster Stanton instructs students not to do their own laundry but to send it out to the new "private cleaning service," as the police have cordoned off the area surrounding the school's laundromat.

FUN

I couldn't keep it inside any longer. There was no way I could *not* tell Nails about Carli Gemz. We were fast approaching the dining hall (fecal burgers and canned peaches! Yum!) and the sun was blazing and—Carli would be there.

I'll really have to call this chick "Sheila Smith." A name my dad invented.

The annual Orientation Luncheon was one of the few Winchester requirements Stanton actually enforced. Under normal circumstances he would grace us with another hackneyed soliloquy about how returning students should make newcomers feel welcome. (Question for Kirk Bishop: Did streaking the dining hall last year make anyone feel welcome, newcomer or veteran?) But given Darcy's disappearance, who knows what he'd say? No doubt he'd make excuses for being such a moron on the radio this morning. And as unfeeling as it sounds, Darcy had once again slipped my mind.

Carli, Carli, Carli, I kept thinking. *Sheila, Sheila, Sheila . . .*

Miraculously, I hadn't seen her yet. Either that or she purposely hadn't tracked me down. I could relate. How had we let my dad talk us into this farce? Oh, right. His nifty new show. My expulsion. Silly me!

Carli could have knocked, I supposed. Nails and I hadn't left our room all morning. We'd been blasting old B-52s so loudly that a bomb could have gone off down the hall and we wouldn't have noticed. Oddly, they were the one band we agreed on.

The trouble started around ten, when we tore open Nails's outlawed coffee machine. He wasn't joking about the "lifters." The stuff wasn't cocaine (I hope), but whatever free samples the International Gourmet Coffee people had included in that box were definitely a little stronger than the average espresso. Within minutes Nails had cued up the deafening music and we were jabbering at each other like two auctioneers: *HEY, do I hear Darcy is dead; HEY, do I hear a kidnapping; HEY, maybe she finally got so sick of this dump of a school that she became a runaway; HEY, do I hear a grisly serial killer; HEY, do I . . . S-O-O-O-L-D: for a random unsolved disappearance.*

"What do you think Stanton will do to Sarah for playing

that tape of him and me?" Nails was asking. "You think he'll shut down WWWW? I still think he planted it."

"Huh?"

All of a sudden, I realized I was wearing an Iron Maiden concert T-shirt. I'd stolen it from Nails last year. Was it hot for September? I was sweating. The dining hall loomed before us, dominating the quad in all its ruined glory. (Picture a state capital with the dome sliced off. Then throw in some crumbling brick and peeling white columns—and carve the word *fidelity* on the portico.) Why hadn't I tagged that ugly-ass building yet? Maybe I'd spray HIGH on the left side of FIDELITY, and CANNED SPEECHES on the right. And underneath: BAD CREDIT? NO CREDIT? NO PROBLEM! FORGET CANNED PEACHES! BUY STANTON'S HI-FI BS!!!

Nails paused on the steps. "Dude, what's the matter with you right now? Have you been listening?"

No, I hadn't. And a lot was the matter, beginning with the parade of insanity shuffling through the double doors. Maybe it was the caffeine crash, but man—how could this place get more depressing? Boys with eyeliner, girls with dyed armpit hair; I longed for a classic New Englander—say, Kirk Bishop, minus the soulless evil and acne. I'd endure the "hell" Sarah once ranted about just to spot a cheerleader. One nice, normal, preppy blond cheerleader. *Go, Winchester. Rah, rah, rah!* Sadly, Darcy Novak was possibly the closest Winchester came to such an ideal, and she was a bohemian freak too. Who knew how Carli Gemz, a.k.a. Sheila Smith, would turn out?

"Nails, I have to tell you something," I heard myself say.

"What? Is it about Darcy?"

"No. We just spent the last two hours on Darcy."

"Yeah, but I thought that was the coffee talking. I can barely stand still. My stomach's making scary noises. One more cup and I'll start to hallucinate."

"We're about to meet someone, Nails," I said gravely.

"What are you talking about? What in the God of name is going on with you?"

"Name of God. We're about to meet a girl named Sheila. But that's not her real name. Her real name is Carli Gemz. Pronounced 'games.'"

Nails placed his bony fingers on my shoulders, his sunken dark eyes boring into my own. "Fun, I know you're tweaked out. I am too. More than you probably even understand. But please come back to planet Earth. We're not about to meet any imaginary friend of yours named Carla Pronounced Games."

"Carli. Not Carla. And she's not imaginary. I mean, she is, but not like you think. We're gonna have to call her Sheila. It's gonna be weird."

His fingers slipped away. "You aren't kidding, are you?"

"No, I'm not. Just let me explain."

And then . . .

It all came pouring out. Maybe it *was* the coffee. I admitted to Nails he'd been right about Charity; I should have been expelled too. But my dad has money and her dad doesn't. Dad directed such classics as *Mr. T: Diary of a Madman* and *My Tummy Hurts: The Seamy Underbelly of America's Eating Contests,* both of which won awards. Or nominations. (Same thing in Hollywood.) So he had the means to buy Stanton off.

I also admitted to Nails—to myself for the first time, really—that Charity might have resented me for this. I confessed that when I'd tried to hang with her this summer, she was a little . . . pissy. So I also explained (meaning *lied*) that *I* was the one who put our relationship on hold. I left out the part about how she blew me off (I didn't want to seem like some clingy wuss). I also left out the part about the Black Eyed Peas video.

For conversation's sake, I did mention that I'd heard a rumor (from my dad, no less), which turned out to be true, that Charity was being shipped off to a new boarding school in Italy to be with her second cousin. A very handsome second cousin, apparently. Some butt-wipe who's shooting an independent feature film "for under two mil!"

So what was I supposed to do, Nails? Share a giddy giggle with the old man about this wonderful news? The old man, who also kindly added that this second cousin was "a better-looking Jude Law type?" Which made me suspect that Charity was already involved in an incestuous romance (based on zero evidence)? That she and this Jude Lawlito probably would get engaged and then married and have inbred babies? That this was her way of coping with the injustice? That I was suffering?

What was I supposed to do, Nails?

Nails stared at me, deeply concerned.

Whatever. I couldn't stop. I blathered on and on. Standing there on the steps of FIDELITY (a word Charity could stand to learn) in that pilfered Iron Maiden concert T, I came clean. (Sort of.) I sought absolution. I let Nails in on the forbidden scoop I'd sworn to take to my grave or graduation, whichever came first. (In fairness to myself, I'd administered this private oath before I'd imbibed Nails's mind-altering coffee.) The bitter truth was: Stanton would only let me graduate if 1) I left my paint cans at home (I didn't); and 2) I served as Carli Gemz's personal assistant and didn't tell a soul (I just had). Only then would I prove to be responsible. As responsible as those demented Winchester souls who didn't vandalize, and therefore were deserving of a diploma.

Nails seemed to be listening. Possibly even getting it. Possibly even forgiving me.

On the other hand, he'd had even more coffee than I had. He looked awful. I can only imagine how gruesome I looked.

I concluded by posing the old rhetorical questions: What *is* vandalism? Some kids (i.e., Kirk Bishop) streak the dining hall on opening day, which is far more inhumane than harmless graffiti. Who wants to see Kirk's pimply butt when you're trying to make new friends and scarf down canned peaches? *That's* vandalism.

Nails tapped his chin. He tapped it for a good long while.

"I don't get it," he said finally. "Why does Carla need a personal assistant at all?"

"Carli. Because it's part of her contract. She's coming to school in character, so she's technically working. And if we can pull the whole thing off, Stanton will get a bonus: a big endowment from my dad's production company, Saint Sancerre Productions. That's the name of the school on the show."

"But isn't that a crime?" he asked. "Like, a real crime? Like blackmail?"

My eyes narrowed. "I don't know. It doesn't matter. Listen, Nails, you can't tell a soul about this. Okay? Only Stanton knows. As far as everyone else is concerned, Carli is Sheila, and I'm just gonna be this sycophantic screwup who makes friends with her. And now that I've told you, I guess you'll have to be friends with her too."

Nails snickered. "Do I have to be sycophantic, too?"

The chapel clock tower began to ring: *DING . . . DING . . .* It was noon, time to enter the dining hall. The last few stragglers scurried inside.

"Fun, I have to tell you something," Nails said slowly. "This whole thing stinks. You once said you'd drop out if Charity got expelled. What are *you* getting out of this? I understand that Stanton gets money and maybe some product placement on your Dad's show. But kids here are going to recognize this chick. She's a famous actress, right?"

I could feel the toxic Winchester grounds collapsing beneath my feet and swallowing me into the earth. "Not that famous," I muttered.

Nails looked me directly in the eye, his sour face stage lit by the noon September sunshine. "You know what?" His voice rose. "Charity *should* be pissed at you."

"Huh?"

"Your dad paid off Stanton to kick her out and keep you in! Charity gets a raw deal because Stanton needs cash! Your family is worse than the Bush Administration! Our pool *is* skankrupt!" He jerked a trembling finger toward the rusted brown statue of

Horace Winchester, smack in the middle of the quad—holding aloft, of all the cruel mockeries, a paintbrush. Once this Carli BS was over, I was gonna tag his ass as well. It was long overdue.

"Yes, Nails, our school is bankrupt," I agreed.

"Morally bankrupt," he said with a sniff. "I bet Carli will earn course credit. Maybe you'll even bang her before she splits."

I frowned. "Hey, why are you so pissed at *me*? I took a huge risk even telling you about her. And I'm not gonna bang her. I can't. My dad made me sign a notarized document stipulating that he can disown me if we have any intimate contact. I'm serious! You want moral bankruptcy? That's how—"

"Is she hot?" Nails interrupted.

"What?"

"Is Carli hot?"

I blinked. "I don't know, sort of."

"Sort of?"

"She's not my type. This is gonna suck, Nails. This is totally gonna suck."

He flashed me a Cheshire-Cat grin. "For you, maybe," he said. "I'm a free man."

Carli

Fun was cuter in person than I expected.

I was hoping—*praying*, was more like it—he'd be cute. I'd been feverishly trying all morning to think "glass half full" about *anything*.

The Winchester School of the Arts was not how I'd imagined it. And I wasn't even that mad at Jonathan Newport anymore, although I did clandestinely text him:

> have u been deleting sheila's email? ok if u have. just wondering.

I left out the part about how Bishop House made Franny's Free-4-All look like Chateau Marmont—how the bathroom sinks were crusty with brown gook. And if Bishop House was a girl's dorm, why were there urinals? Sheila's dorm at St. Sancerre didn't have urinals. St. Sancerre was a paradise. Or it was in the first draft of the first script.

By lunchtime I was desperate. I needed an activity, a distraction. Where was my personal assistant?

It didn't help that Miranda was kind of a Chatty Cathy. I couldn't get a word in, so I retreated back into the darkness of my brain. One of the first things I learned at the soup kitchen is to let strangers ramble on in uncomfortable situations. You don't even have to listen. Sometimes it's best that you *don't*. You can just smile sympathetically and nod, particularly if the stranger is relating something personal or inappropriate or just plain bizarre. Most times, people are just looking for a sounding board anyway.

So I suppose from the glass-half-full angle, the more she got on my nerves, the better it was for my character. (Everyone gets on Sheila Smith's nerves, even when she gets her way.)

Miranda seemed bent on playing detective as we trekked across campus. "Here's the path that leads through the old vineyards toward the laundry, where Darcy Novak was last seen by her ex . . . interesting because it's close to the arts building. Darcy was a theater person . . . so maybe she could have been hanging out in the arts building before she vanished? What do you think? It's a possibility. Clues, clues . . ."

I couldn't bring myself to think about some girl I'd never met. Mostly, I thought about how the entire campus needed a sprucing up. Those *Bulletin* pictures were definitely Photoshopped. I'd counted three boarded-up windows by the time we pushed through the big double doors of the dining hall.

Then I froze.

Two sweaty boys in black T-shirts stood in the passageway. They turned.

"Sheila?" one of them asked.

Oh, my—

My prayers had been answered. Here I was, face to face with Fun.

My pulse picked up a notch. I reminded myself, *Remember why you're here. To meet lots of weird, bad, naughty people.* I would channel every ounce of annoyance and depression into Sheila Smith, and . . . Oh, who was I trying to fool? I would just end up more annoyed and depressed by faking my way through this school for the next three weeks with a rude jerk at my side. It was like a prison sentence. How would I get along with someone who spray-painted everything in sight? No matter how noble his intentions?

"Fun, right?" I asked in the cheeriest voice I could manage.

"Yeah," he said. "Hi."

Miranda wrinkled her forehead. Her eyes darted back and forth between us.

"Nice to see you," I said.

It was a line I'd rehearsed three dozen plus times on the flight from LA. It came out flat. *Glass half full, Glass half full* . . . I focused on the positives. He *was* decent-looking. Blond and blue eyed, not too tall . . . and thankfully, not nearly as frightening as his skim-milk-colored friend, whose haunting eyes made him look as if he'd just risen from the grave. I was used to guys giving me the once-over in LA, but this was different. He stared at me the way a feral kitten might stare at a mouse.

"Nice to see you too, Sheila," Fun said. He glanced at Miranda.

"Oh, Miranda, I'm sorry! This is Fellini Newport. His friends call him Fun. His dad and mine are old friends. We're both from LA. My dad told me I should look up Fun when I got here, so he could show me the ropes—you know, since he's been here for such a long time." I don't think I've ever delivered anything that sounded so lame and stilted, not even at my worst audition. "Four years, right?"

"Three years, Sheila," he replied dully. "Three."

"He got kicked out of Choate first," his friend cut in. He spoke with a New York accent. "I'm Fun's roommate, by the way. Call me Nails."

Miranda giggled. "Why should we call you Nails?"

He lifted his bony shoulders. "I'm handy with tools. Fun here is handy with paint. He's a real graffiti artist! But after enough run-ins with the cops, his dad got a little fed up." He nudged Fun in the ribs and smiled broadly. "You've probably heard those stories a million times, right, Sheila?"

"What's your real name, Nails?" Miranda asked out of nowhere.

"Hilton James," he said. "Why?"

"Nothing. It's just I think I heard your name on the school radio this morning—"

"We should be getting into the dining hall," Fun interrupted. He wiped his forehead with the back of his palm. "Sorry, as new students, you two owe it to yourselves to hear Stanton. It's . . . um, high comedy."

Miranda's face fell. "But a girl is missing. She's my dorm counselor!"

Uh-oh. I swallowed. Nails's shoulders sagged. He squeezed his purple-rimmed eyes shut and rubbed them with his palms. "She's *my* ex-girlfriend," he mumbled.

"She is?" I gasped.

"Let's talk about it later," Fun urged. "Come on. We're late." He hurried across the common room toward the dining-hall door, adding yet another trail of sneaker prints to the dingy yellow wall-to-wall carpet.

Miranda rushed after them. I followed a few paces behind.

My head spun. Nails was the missing senior girl's ex-boyfriend. He could be a dangerous psychopath. He certainly looked the part. My breathing grew labored. No wonder Fun was so rude. I would be rude too, if I went to this school. I could feel myself *turning* rude, a good thing, I reminded myself, in terms of my character. But it also reminded me of something Dr. Fein once told me: There's a point every actress reaches when she knows there's no point in trying to fool herself anymore. I'd reached it.

Especially when I entered the cafeteria. The air inside smelled. It *stank*.

Not like the soup kitchen, either. It reeked of burned meat, with just the faintest whiff of boiled vegetables. If I'd been depressed earlier, I don't know what I was now. Even the décor was sad. Formica lunch tables, summer-camp-style, packed into a vast, dark, mahogany-walled room—a room that might have housed nicer furniture during better times but now looked like a Salvation Army warehouse. And the students! *I* was the one who was supposed to be in disguise. But even at the seediest Hollywood parties, I'd never seen so many pierced noses or black nail polish or secondhand clothing. This couldn't prepare me for St. Sancerre. We weren't making a show about boot camp.

Headmaster Stanton stood at a lectern in the back of the cafeteria, directly in front of a steaming buffet. A nervous smile played on his lips.

With his gray hair not-so-professionally slicked back and his belly oozing from a tie-less suit, I wondered if he was trying to appear fatherly.

"Winchester, nothing matters more to me or to the rest of the faculty than your safety," he stated. "The Wellington police have cordoned off the area where Darcy Novak was last seen, pending the investigation. Our laundry facility has been temporarily closed. We've hired a laundry service, based in Wellington, to handle your needs. Laundry bags are to be left in neat piles in your dorm common areas each Friday morning. They will be delivered to you promptly the following Monday morning before classes. Let me make this doubly clear: The area by the laundry facility is off-limits until further notice. Corleone Cleaners will provide service from now on . . ."

Wait. Did he say 'Corleone Cleaners'?

My eyes began to sting.

For a second, I was worried I might start crying. Corleone was the name of the family in *The Godfather*, my parents' favorite movie.

This was it. Three hours in, and I'd already reached the breaking point. I bolted back into the deserted common area, fumbling for my cell phone. I could feel Fun and Miranda and Nails staring at me. I tried to ignore them. I needed to call home. I needed to talk to Mom and Dad. I needed to be grounded. Not "grounded" grounded (though that wouldn't have been so bad; at least I wouldn't be *here*)—grounded as in getting both feet firmly planted back in the familiar.

I jabbed at the keypad and drew in a shaky breath.

Pick up, pick up, I begged, leaning against a fingerprint-stained pillar.

Mom answered after the first ring. "Sweetie! Hi! Did you make it to Winchester okay? Jonathan Newport called to say that the chauffeur—"

"Mom, the cleaning service here is named Corleone," I interrupted breathlessly. "You know? Like from *The Godfather*?"

There was a long silence.

"Mom?" I croaked, my voice trembling.

"Let me get your father, dear," she said. "He's much better at handling this movie-trivia stuff than I am."

Another line clicked. "Carli? Sweetheart? Is everything okay?"

"No! Well . . . I don't know. This place is really weird. A girl has disappeared. She was supposed to be my dorm advisor. Everybody looks like a delinquent. And the cleaning service is named after the family from *The Godfather*—"

"Shh," Dad soothed. "Slow down, Carli. You're just homesick. It's natural."

I frowned. "Dad, a girl is missing! She was kidnapped or something! My roommate is already flipping out! It's a big deal!"

Dad took a deep breath. "I'll ask Jonathan about it, okay?"

"What do you think *he* can do?"

"Listen, darling," Mom piped up. "If you're feeling stressed, why don't you do something nice for someone? Like Dr. Fein says: Climb out of your shame cellar."

I groaned. "Shame *spiral*, Mom."

"Right, right, of course. You know what I mean. Tell a stranger that his or her shoes are untied. It can be something that small. It's a great way to make new friends! You're always so good at finding little faults in everyone and helping out. It always makes you feel so much better."

"Yes, but not in an overbearing way," Dad added.

"Of course not," Mom agreed. "The best part is that it makes the people you help feel better too. No good deed goes unpunished!"

"No bad deed, honey," Dad corrected. "So Carli, have you met with your new personal assistant yet? I can ask Jonathan about that . . ."

I squeezed my eyes closed. *Bad idea to call home.* "I'm sorry, guys. I gotta go. I'm not supposed to use my cell phone except for emergencies."

"Carli?" Mom and Dad both asked at the same time.

"Bye!" I hung up and shoved the phone into my pocket, racing back into the dining hall. I smiled at Nails, Fun, and Miranda.

"Please come forward if you have any information at all that might help us find Darcy," Headmaster Stanton pleaded from the rear. "If you're frightened of incriminating yourself in some way, don't be. We'll give you a pass. What matters is finding her."

"Why are you smiling like that?" Nails asked me. "You think this is humorous?"

The color drained from my face. "No, I . . . I don't know. Headmaster Stanton sounds like a Muppet." It was the first thing that popped into my head. "Or someone who's just breathed in, like, a big balloon of helium. Doesn't he?"

For some reason, this struck Fun as funny. He started laughing. He laughed so hard that Stanton stopped talking. He laughed so hard that every single kid in the dining hall turned to look at us, standing in the entranceway—the last four students to arrive on the tragic opening day of the new Winchester school year. At that moment, I truly was Sheila Smith. I would have to thank Fun later for helping me get into character. For now, however, I wanted to be Carli. I was on a mission. Why be depressed? Mom was right. I was homesick, sure. But at root, the only reason I was depressed was because of the shame. My eyes drifted across the sea of faces . . . and I sought out the loneliest, ugliest, saddest looking of the bunch, someone even worse than Nails. And . . .

Bingo! As soon as I spotted those pimples, I knew I had my work cut out for me. I would turn that frown upside down.

3

Carli meets some of the more dubious members of the Winchester faculty and student body. Later, Fun and Carli share an ambiguous moment.

Fun

Carli does possess a wretched-if-saintly obsession with jerks in need of help. It walks hand in hand with her great talent for sidling up to them and insinuating herself into their lives. God knows what compels her. And watching her make a beeline for Kirk Bishop's table that day, I couldn't help thinking about her previous personal assistant. Before I'd left for Winchester, Dad showed me Grizz's police record.

His real name was Earl Griswald. In 1986, he was jailed for hurling a wrench at his twelve-year-old nephew. (He missed.) Apparently, the boy preferred Kiss's original drummer to the replacement. Dad also showed me an e-mail Carli had sent soon after they'd begun negotiations for *Private Nights.*

> jonathan . . . don't worry about grizz's conviction . . . the wrench thing was over 20 yrs ago . . . he is such a sweetie now . . . he hasn't been arrested since! ☺

How nice. During the intervening two decades, Earl Griswald had violated his parole and lived on the lam, only to magically reappear in the soup kitchen where Carli volunteered—bloated, knife-scarred, and homeless—as "a sweetie." No wonder Carli included the smiley face. What a happy ending! From that perspective, it made sense that she plopped down beside Kirk. Appearance-wise, Kirk made Nails look like a poster child for healthy living.

It makes no sense that Darcy would ever dump Nails for Kirk. Was there a side to Kirk we'd all missed? He'd deteriorated over the summer. His hair was stringier, his clothes were shabbier, and his acne had spread. His face was also a strange pinkish orange. Not from a suntan. I doubted he'd gone to the beach. The last time we'd seen him he'd told Nails and me (we hadn't asked) that he planned to spend every single day "from June to September inside, blowing [his] mind out."

Maybe Darcy felt drawn to undesirables too. Maybe she and Carli were alike.

Nails chuckled.

"What could possibly be funny?" I asked.

"You're a liar," he whispered.

"I am?" Something about his tone struck me as slightly off.

"You said that Carli was 'sort of' hot." He wriggled his eyebrows. "Dude, she's smoking. I love pigtails. Like I said, I need to find a hot new senior transfer. This fake chick of yours is right up my alley."

My face twisted in a grimace. I shot an anxious glance toward Miranda, but she hadn't heard us, or maybe she was just pretending to not listen. She stared at Carli, who beckoned, silently mouthing, "COME ON," as if we were all old pals, as if lunching with Kirk Bishop on the first day of school was perfectly natural.

Worse, Kirk wasn't alone. Sarah Ryder and Mary Fishman sat with him.

Since when would Sarah Ryder consider sitting with Kirk? She hated him as much as we did. She hated everybody except Mary, and maybe even Mary, too. Or she used to . . . but that was back when she had eyebrow piercings. And purple lip gloss. Now Sarah was practically unrecognizable. She was wearing a pantsuit. A freaking pinstriped black *pantsuit*, like the kind a corporate secretary would wear.

At least she hadn't tossed her long-suffering sidekick. Yes, Proud Mary had tagged along with Sarah from day one of freshman year—though to call them "friends" would be pushing it. I'd rarely seen them speak. Outwardly, Mary also went the way of the angry, black-clad Goth, as Sarah once had. (*Her* eyebrow piercings were still intact.) Inwardly, she remained a deliberate enigma. And as per tradition, she was scribbling very furiously and publicly in her diary. I almost felt comforted. Here, finally, was someone who hadn't undergone a massive transformation over the summer.

"Come *on*!" Carli cried.

I'm trapped, I thought in a mild panic.

The three of us shambled over and slumped down in the empty folding chairs at the end of the table. I flashed a weak grin at our lunch-mates.

Sarah smiled back from the head of the table. Very strange. Smiling was to Sarah what right-wing politics was to Nails: an anathema.

"Hi Fun," she whispered, taking a bite of her burger.

I waved uneasily.

"Well, it's nure shice to—I mean, sure nice to see everyone," Nails proclaimed. "Hey, Sarah, how's tricks? Quick thing I wanted to ask you: How the hell did you get your hands on that recording of Stanton and me?"

I winced.

Sarah arched an eyebrow. "You know I can't reveal my sources, Nails."

"Of course not! Well. So. Enough about that. How was everyone's summer?"

Kirk leered at Carli and Miranda. "I don't remember mine," he mumbled. He hunched over his plate and seized his burger. "Who are your new friends, Nails?"

"I'm Sheila Smith," Carli answered. "This is Miranda Jenkins."

"Classy names, classy dames," Kirk replied in a pseudo-rap. "I'm Kirk."

Dames. I imagined what it would feel like to snatch up Kirk's knife, smear it with ketchup, and write LUCIFER on his forehead with it. I imagined the whole dining hall erupting in a standing ovation. I even imagined Stanton applauding. I wasn't as deft with ketchup as I was with spray paint, but I could make it work.

"How about you, Mary?" Nails asked. "Oh, Sheila and Miranda, this is Mary Fishman. She writes novels. Or so she claims. Luckily, her only source is herself."

Mary glanced up at Nails and me, then at our T-shirts. "Iron Maiden and James Brown," she remarked in a robotic monotone. "Cute." She turned back to her notebook.

"Well, we *were* listening to the B-52s earlier," Nails replied defensively. "Hey Car—I mean, Sheila. Do you like the B-52s?"

Carli shrugged. Miranda let out a tired little laugh. I wondered then if she knew who Carli really was, because I noticed something: Little crow's-feet formed at the edges of her eyes. They made her seem older and more world-weary than the rest of us. Then again, it could have been the company. These people were lunatics, the conversation was off-kilter, and nobody really seemed to give a crap that Darcy Novak had disappeared.

I don't know why, but I suffered an Insta-Crush right then.

If you say you've never had an Insta-Crush—those split-second bouts of dizzying infatuation with a stranger—you're a liar. (Admittedly, horny young males are most susceptible.) There is no rational explanation. But it comes on fast, like a coffee buzz.

Without a shred of evidence, I instantly believed Miranda's crow's-feet offered a promise of something profound, of a soul. I thought, *We need Miranda at Winchester.* I should paint her portrait on some wall and capture her weariness and sensitivity. I *would* paint it, because her whole earnest vibe stood in direct opposition to everyone else at the table.

Uh-oh.

The Insta-Crush screeched to a halt.

Sarah was studying Carli with a strange intensity. She chewed her hamburger at a glacial pace. Maybe she was a closet fan of *Deadbeat Dad.*

"You look different, Sarah," I said, just to distract her. "You look great!"

"Oh, don't worry," she said with her mouth full. Her eyes remained pinned on Carli. "I'm still an asshole. I'm just dressing this way because I need to get into college."

"Smart move," Nails said.

Mary laughed wickedly, scribbling. She hadn't touched her lunch. Last year, Nails theorized that Mary Fishman didn't actually write anything in her diary other than a tribute to *The Shining*: ALL WORK AND NO PLAY MAKES MARY A DULL GIRL . . . ALL WORK AND NO PLAY MAKES MARY A DULL GIRL . . .

"Nails, I thought you wanted to know what I was working on," she said.

"Absolutely," he replied. "I wish Sarah was a little more forthcoming, but . . ."

"It's the beginning of a novel." Mary took a deep breath and read aloud: "Do you know my dad? Sure you do. Everyone knows my dad. Maybe he's your dad, too. The touchy-feely dad who decides to become headmaster of a boarding school? The dad who lets teenage girls slip through his fingers? Is that your dad?"

I turned to Carli and Miranda. Their faces were stricken.

"So Sarah, where are you applying to college?" My voice squeaked. "I—"

"Fun!" Sarah dropped her burger on her plate. "Darcy Novak is missing. Darcy Novak—a wild talent, a friend of everyone at this table except these new transfers, an intimate partner to some—is gone. And you want to know where I'm *applying*?"

I blinked. A hard lump formed in my throat.

"I never knew you and Darcy were so close, Sarah," Nails commented.

Sarah sighed. "I respected Darcy. Everyone grieves differently, Nails."

"Word," Kirk said in mid-chew. "I'm so messed up I don't even plan on taking classes this year." Little bits of hamburger escaped from his lips as he spoke.

Lord, get me out of here.

Maybe Nails's wild conspiracy theory was correct and Stanton was responsible for leaking the recording of that interrogation. Maybe Sarah was screwing with us all. Or maybe she *was* grieving. Maybe she'd changed. God bless her.

I wondered if Kirk would ever change, if he would ever experience enough pain or acquire enough wisdom to develop crow's-feet. Doubtful. There was no reason for Kirk to reinvent himself. Nothing bad could ever happen to him here; he was untouchable. Nobody would set *him* up or use him as a patsy. His great-grandfather had given the school so much money that the trustees named a dorm after the family—back when students still plucked grapes from the vineyard and used the old distillery to brew their own homemade rotgut. Why shouldn't he continue to be depraved and callous? Even with a missing girlfriend?

Life must be nice for him, I thought. I pushed away from the table and headed for the buffet. *God bless him, too. God bless his acne and his moral-free, soulless existence!*

Carli

I spent the rest of the afternoon alone. I told Miranda that I still needed to figure out what extracurricular activities I wanted to get involved with.

I lied.

In truth, I was looking for any excuse to be by myself—as far as possible from my new roommate, from Fun and Nails, from Evil Pantsuit and Mad Pimple Boy and Diary Girl. Okay, it wasn't a *complete* lie. I did wander over to the administration building, basically a crumbling replica of the house in *Addams Family Values*. There I curled up on a worn sofa and pored over various brochures and the school's course guide. I must have scoured every piece of printed matter Winchester had to offer . . . just for a single club that wasn't devoted to a niche interest—one that didn't involve *a cappella* singing or

Web design or mime or yoga . . . a single club devoted to *helping other people.*

Nada. Zilch. The closest one I found was "Students for a Democratic Society." As far as I could tell, they existed solely to boycott all the other clubs—for reasons I couldn't quite figure out. Not surprisingly Nails was a member.

I didn't get it. My old public school in LA, lame as it was, offered plenty of opportunities to snap out of a shame spiral. You could participate in food drives or campaign for UNICEF. You could intern at a hospital. You could join "Peers Helping Peers," a big outreach program where volunteers took anonymous phone calls from fellow students coping with serious problems. But I guess as far as an outreach program like that went, Winchester was covered. As I learned that afternoon, over half the faculty doubled as shrinks for the student body.

Still, it wasn't a total wash: I did decide on a class schedule. I figured I should be as creative as possible, since I wasn't going to receive any credit on my real-life transcript. And boy was I creative! An old woman in a Shetland sweater and bifocals printed out the final version for me. We were the last two people left in the building.

"Better run along now, dear," she lisped through her dentures. "It's suppertime!"

I glanced down at the sheet.

PERIOD ONE 9:15–10:05 am: History of Advertising

PERIOD TWO 10:20–11:15 am: Mirth and Modern Cinema

PERIOD THREE 11:30 am–12:15 pm: Abstract Sculpture

** Lunch **

PERIOD FOUR 1:15–2:00 pm: How to Write an Effective Haiku

Period FIVE 2:15–3:00 pm: Broadcast Journalism

Period SIX 3:15–4:00 pm: What Makes Cartoons Funny

How on earth will any of this help me to become Sheila Smith?

I thanked her and shoved the paper in my pocket.

A breeze rustled my hair as I trudged across the quad to the dining hall. Crickets chirped. The sun sank below the horizon. At the top of the steps, I glanced over my shoulder at the campus. Incredible. At this hour, with the quiet, in the fading light, Winchester almost managed to look pretty.

This isn't so bad, I thought to myself. I pushed through the big double doors. *Only three weeks, right? I can handle three weeks.*

My nose wrinkled.

The place smelled even worse than it had at lunch. I poked my head inside the cafeteria. It was the land time forgot; nobody appeared to have left. I felt a wave of depression, hearing the same joyless drone of hushed conversation, seeing the same sea of thrown-together outfits and unkempt hair—

"Sheila!" a voice cried.

Miranda bolted up from a table by the buffet and waved me over.

Depression turned to misery. Seated with her was that same lunchtime crew I'd sought to avoid: Fun, Nails, Mad Pimple Boy,

Evil Pantsuit, and Diary Girl. It was truly déjà vu—except that instead of burgers, they were now feasting upon what looked like Depression-era stew, brownish slop with chunks of carrots, and cubes of meat.

I would definitely go without dinner tonight.

"Hey, where have you been?" Miranda asked as I slumped at the far end of the table. "I was starting to get worried."

"Uh . . . at the administration building," I mumbled. "Trying to find clubs to join."

"Very diligent of you, Sheila," Fun said in a dry voice. "Kudos."

"Thanks, but it wasn't a huge success."

"Dude!" Mad Pimple Boy cried. "If you're looking for a club to join, you should join us! The Book Society! We have a great reading list this year. We're starting with *The Human Stain*, by Philip Roth. Ever read it?"

I laughed in spite of myself. "Are you talking to me?"

"Yeah?"

"I'm a dude?"

He chuckled. "We're all dudes. I'm for equal opportunity. Power to the people."

"Right on, dude!" Nails murmured. He cast a quick sidelong glance at me, his face softening, as if to silently apologize for Kirk. Maybe he *wasn't* so damaged. I even caught a glimpse of humanity in those purple-rimmed pupils, just the way I'd caught it in Grizz that first day at Franny's. I quashed the pang of homesickness.

"Can I join the Book Society too?" Fun asked.

"I don't know," Evil Pantsuit grumbled. "Can you?"

"Sarah, be nice," Nails said. "Don't fun judge—"

"Fun judge?" she interrupted with a wicked smile. She stirred her bowl. "Thanks, Nails. Good advice. But by telling me what to do, you're judging *me*. You're being a hypocrite. Let him who is without sin cast the first stone."

"Amen," Diary Girl chimed in.

Nails slumped in his chair. "Oh, brother. Here we go. That would be the Bible, wouldn't it? Didn't you read that during a Book Society meeting? Darcy told me that you guys read all the classics."

"How would you know anything about the Book Society, Nails?" Mad Pimple Boy asked.

"You really want to go there, Kirk?" Nails replied evenly.

Mad Pimple Boy tilted his head at Nails, frozen and dangerous, like a guard dog. I bristled. I knew that stare. Everybody knows it, or should: It's in all kinds of classic films (e.g., *The Godfather)*. It's the stare of a vicious male right before he attacks or says something he'll regret. For a split second, I considered bolting. But that wouldn't solve anything. It would just send me back inside my own head, bad for both me *and* Sheila. Tomorrow I'd still have to deal with the ugliness and tension; I'd have to deal with it for as long as I was stuck here—unless I wanted to call it quits.

Enough. Dr. Fein was right; I had to be active, and I had to tell the truth whenever possible. I'd spent all afternoon feeling sorry for myself, searching for a way to get involved. Right now it was staring me in the face. Everyone at this table needed help.

Maybe even more than Grizz had. I should lend a hand. Being an outsider, a newcomer, might even help. I could be detached, professional. After all, I didn't know Darcy Novak. I wasn't emotionally invested in her. That distance could help me help *them* work through their feelings about her. Because I was certain that she lay at the heart of all this weirdness. Two of the three guys sitting here had *dated* her—two guys who seemed on the verge of killing each other.

"Sheila?" Fun asked. "Are you okay?"

"Yeah. I was just thinking. How about we all join the Book Society?" I gestured to Fun, Nails, and Miranda. "Everybody here should join!"

Kirk laughed flatly. "Are you serious?"

I nodded. "Yeah. Is that cool?"

He shrugged, turning to Sarah and Mary.

"Dude!" Nails cried, smiling widely. "That is a *great* idea. Don't you think so, Fun? I need more extracurricular activities anyway. SDS doesn't cut it. Count me in."

Fun shifted in his seat. Mary and Sarah stared uncomfortably into their bowls of stew. I held my breath.

"The Book Society will improve my failing vocabulary, too," Nails added. "You know what? I'm never going to use the word *dude* again. It's a terrible word."

Miranda laughed and touched his arm. "I totally agree! I hate that word, too." She smiled apologetically at Kirk, her fingers lingering on Nails's skin. Her fingers began creeping down toward his wrist. "No offense."

Kirk shrugged, the spell broken. He dove back into his dinner.

"None taken. Welcome to the Book Society. This will be great. Thanks, Sheila."

"Yeah, thanks," Nails said. With that, he clamped his hand over Miranda's.

I blinked.

Nails and Miranda are holding hands.

Only Fun seemed to notice. He turned to me. Then he quickly turned back to them, his eyebrows tightly knit. I wondered if he was thinking what I was thinking: What the hell was going on here? Couples didn't form that fast, not even back in LA. Was Nails trying to prove to everyone that he was over Darcy? If he was, I supposed that would explain Kirk's strange look of contentment; it might even explain why Sarah and Mary were choosing to ignore this public display of affection, as well. Was Miranda some kind of nymphomaniac? It was a possibility; she *had* hooked up with her gym teacher . . . or maybe she was looking for a way to forget about Darcy Novak, too.

"Thank you for taking us to Karmageddon, Sheila," Nails said, apropos of nothing. "I'm very pleased."

I swallowed. "Thanks for taking you where?"

"Karmageddon. It's a made-up word I found in a newspaper this summer. It's the apocalypse that ensues when a bunch of nutcases reach a critical mass of bad vibes. And I'm pretty sure that's where we're headed if we're all in the Book Society."

Fun

Amazing: I almost managed to forget about how pissed I was at being Carli's slave. I almost forgot about *everything*, except for the burning question screaming for an immediate answer.

Why was Nails holding hands with Carli's roommate?

"I could really go for dessert right now," I announced. "Nails? Care to join me?"

"No thanks," he said, smiling into Miranda's eyes.

"Why don't you just finish mine?" Mary asked absently, scribbling away in her diary. She nodded toward a half-eaten bowl of Jell-O. "If we're all going to be in the Book Society together, we should learn to share."

Kirk chuckled. "That's the spirit—" He broke off and groaned. "Oh, crap. Here comes Stanton."

Sure enough, Stanton was waddling over to our table, accompanied by Mr. Hines, the head of the drama department. Mr. Hines was another Winchester "lifer," a single, balding, cadaverous father of two elflike toddlers who often roamed the campus naked. He moonlighted as chief of campus security. I'd never been able to get a grip on him. Was he gay? (Not that I cared.) But what happened to his wife? Who was she? And why had she married a lame drama teacher in the first place? Why hadn't she taken their kids with her when she'd escaped this awful place?

At least Stanton was pretend-happily married to Eliza Stanton, a wrinkled brunette zero who preferred to spend fall semesters "away from campus." (Read: "having an affair.") Their three adult kids were scattered across the country. In other words, Stanton had reached that blissful point in life where he was off the hook, family-wise. I was almost jealous of him. My family obligations bound me to Carli, who'd just forced me into the goddamn Book

Society. I couldn't let her join *alone*.

"Hello, everyone," Stanton greeted us soberly. "Quite a day, eh?" He frowned at my T-shirt, then at Nails's T-shirt. "Gentlemen, I know the dress code was abolished in 1974, but there needs to be a modicum . . . of . . . of . . ."

"Of booty up in this piece," Kirk Bishop finished.

"What was that, Kirk?"

"Booty," Kirk said. "A modicum of booty. Sorry for the slang, but I aim to play Danny in *Grease* this year. *Modicum* means 'small portion,' right? I took that SAT course you recommended this summer, Stanton." He flashed a yellow grin at Nails, who quickly withdrew his hand from Miranda's. "Check my man Nails over there. He's got the right idea. He's pimping! Get what I'm saying, hoss?"

"Not really," Stanton said quietly. "But I'm happy you took the SAT course."

I glanced at Carli. I wondered what was running through her head. Horror? Bewilderment? A combination thereof?

I should have explained some things to her about Winchester. Namely: Stanton and Kirk's unique relationship. It was simple. Stanton relied on money from the Bishop family to help run the school, so he tolerated Kirk's psychotic behavior. In turn, Kirk was at his most outrageously foulmouthed around Stanton, because he could get away with it.

Too bad Darcy wasn't here. She understood the Stanton/Bishop rapport too. Or she used to. We used to joke about it, even—back when she and Nails were dating.

For the zillionth time, I wondered what prompted the breakup. She used to tell me that my dad should create a TV show based on Stanton and Kirk: A freakish father whose least-favorite son is a screwup but still keeps the old man afloat. I started to feel sick, and it wasn't the stew. I missed Darcy more than ever. I was *angry* at her. I wanted to grab her in the flesh and demand to know why she'd lost her mind.

"Hey, Mr. Hines, you've seen the movie version of *Grease*, right?" Nails asked.

"Yes, I've seen it, Hilton," Mr. Hines said. "I'm directing our production."

Nails nodded. "Well, I'm just thinking out loud here, but doesn't the bad guy in the movie have tons of zits? Kirk might be better suited for *that* role than the lead."

The table sat silently, poised for Kirk to fire back some offensive put-down. Instead, his lips began to quiver. His eyes moistened. He dropped his spoon in the bowl of stew. It clanked loudly on the rim. A single tear fell from his mottled cheek.

"Who would *Darcy* play, Nails?" he whispered, his voice shaking.

"Kirk?" Mary asked. She closed her notebook. "Are you okay?"

Without a word, he jumped up and stormed out of the dining hall.

"Kirk!" Stanton shouted after him. He whirled and glared at Nails. "What's going on between you two? And Sarah, I've been meaning to talk to you. How—"

"Headmaster Stanton?" Carli piped up. "I'm sorry to interrupt, but I wanted to introduce myself. I realize this probably isn't the best time, but I wasn't sure when I'd get another chance. I'm Sheila Smith. You know? The new transfer from LA?"

He blinked at her. "Pardon?"

"Sheila Smith," she repeated.

"Oh." He stiffened. "Yes. Sheila Smith. Yes, you."

"And this is my roommate, Miranda."

"Listen, it's nice to meet you two, but I have to . . ."

He didn't bother to finish. He was already halfway out the door, scurrying fast in Kirk Bishop's wake with Mr. Hines close on his heels. I stared at their big vanishing butts. (I admit, I was thinking, *Booty*.) My brain began to squirm. That was a pretty fast getaway. Ha! Perhaps Hines and Stanton were worried that Kirk would disappear too. Darcy Novak was bad enough, but a Bishop? They couldn't afford that.

I actually found myself wishing the cops had hung around. If anybody needed interrogating, it was Mr. Hines. As head of security, wasn't he legally responsible for Darcy Novak's disappearance? Then again, he was nothing but an overgrown child, same as Stanton. They couldn't be held responsible for anything. Running away like that? It was beyond rude; it was beyond pitiful. It was *craven*. They used Kirk's meltdown as an excuse to escape Carli, nothing more. Stanton didn't want to face the Faustian bargain he'd forged with my father. I could understand his motive, but at least he should have the decency—a "modicum" of manners—to make Carli feel welcome.

Maybe I'd underestimated her. The girl had guts. It took guts to come here, obviously. But it also took guts to call Stanton on his BS within three seconds of meeting him. It took guts to shove our collective secret right in his face.

"Wow," Sarah said. "Intense."

Miranda looked around the table. "Yeah," she said. "Intense."

Nails took her hand again.

This is too much. Why Nails continued to hit on this girl was beyond me. If he was trying to prove to everyone that he was over Darcy, he was definitely overcompensating. But there was no point in driving myself any crazier. All I knew was that I didn't feel like sitting at the table.

So I didn't. I pulled a Kirk Bishop. I hopped up and ran for the exit.

Carli

Later that night, alone with Miranda in our cramped little room, I stewed.

Sleep was out of the question. The mattress was too lumpy. My comforter wasn't thick enough. I hated this place. How could Fun have left me alone at dinner like that? What a lame move! Didn't I deserve a little credit for scaring Headmaster Stanton off? And what about joining the Book Society? Fun should have known that I'd done it to start a healing process. A blind person could see that he and his crew of wackos needed be healed. Immediately. This Darcy Novak business was a cancer, eating away at them.

Or maybe he was just a jerk.

Evidence: He'd dated Charity Barker. Too bad; I thought I'd gotten a good read on him. Then again, I thought I'd gotten a good read on Miranda. *Ugh.* I could hear her tossing and turning in her own bed, not ten feet away. Talk about major self-esteem issues. Talk about "a slut with no morals." (Okay, I hate the word *slut*; it's harsh—I'm just quoting Fun.) But why was she throwing herself at Nails? Plus, she was so emotionally fragile. Crying over some girl she'd never even met? Not a good sign . . . although I must say, my own curiosity about Darcy had been piqued.

"Hey, Sheila?" Miranda whispered in the darkness.

"Yeah?"

"What do *you* think happened to Darcy Novak?"

"Funny. I was just thinking about her. I don't know. Maybe she wised up and ran away. Maybe she was sick of this place."

"You really think Winchester is that bad?" Miranda asked.

I closed my eyes. "Well . . . no," I lied. "She could have gone to a friend's, I guess. Maybe she just decided to freshen up a little, to pick out a new wardrobe. Maybe that's why she had the sack of laundry. She could have been sneaking off to trade her clothes in for something new. You know, to start over."

"Start over," Miranda echoed. "Is that what you want to do?"

"Some of the time," I said. It's easier to tell the truth when the lights are out.

"Me too," Miranda said. "But no way did Darcy go to a friend's. She was supposed to check us in last night. She wouldn't have missed that. Responsibility was her *thing.*"

"Yeah, but if she was so responsible, how come you got a welcome-to-school e-mail from her, and I didn't?" I asked. Obviously it was an unfair question. I knew the answer, and it had nothing to do with Darcy Novak or her responsibility. It had to do with my new boss, screwing with my head, three thousand miles away.

"It must have been a glitch in the system," Miranda replied.

A glitch in the system, I silently agreed. *Winchester's entire system is made up of glitches. A girl has been missing for more than forty-eight hours. They say if a crime isn't solved in the first forty-eight hours, chances are it won't ever be. And no matter how twisted the students or creepy the faculty or lax the rules, that is plain WRONG.*

"Good night, Sheila," Miranda said.

"Good night."

For several minutes I stared up at the ceiling. Darcy should have been there to wish us good night too. Instead, our dorm advisor—Miss George, a short pixielike redhead just out of college—had. "Be safe," she'd said.

Nice. I didn't *feel* safe. Darcy's room was right above ours, the lone single on the third floor, a converted attic. The police had taped off the stairwell to block access. It occurred to me then that they hadn't returned since. Why not? Wasn't her room just as likely as the laundry facility to provide a clue to her whereabouts . . . maybe even more so?

I held my breath, listening to Miranda. Her own breathing had settled into a loud, even rhythm. She was asleep.

As quietly as possible, I tiptoed out of the room and closed the door behind me.

I wasn't even fully conscious of what I was doing until I ducked under the yellow tape with CAUTION: DO NOT CROSS on it and crept up the stairs.

To my surprise, Darcy's door was unlocked. I pushed it open and inched inside, shivering. My teeth chattered. It wasn't even cold. The light trickling in from the second floor didn't illuminate much—except that Darcy was a neat freak. Perfectly organized bookshelf, perfectly made bed, perfectly folded sweaters atop a locked trunk . . . a poster of Olivia Newton-John in *Grease,* perfectly centered over her desk. I nearly smiled.

I flicked on the desk lamp, taking a moment to blink and squint as my eyes adjusted. Nothing here, either—just a couple of unopened notebooks, a laptop, and a mug full of pens. On a whim I opened the drawer.

My body tensed.

There was a lone envelope inside. Scribbled on the front was a single word: NAILS. *Jesus.* The police must have missed this. I glanced over my shoulder toward the door. My pulse started to quicken.

I shouldn't do this. I shouldn't do this. I shouldn't—

But from a certain point of view, I wasn't even here. Sheila Smith was. And Sheila Smith would have no qualms about reading someone else's mail. And it wasn't stamped, so technically it wasn't mail, anyway, right?

Fingers trembling, I tore it open and pulled out the contents. The envelope fluttered to the floor.

Dear Nails,

I feel sort of funny writing you a letter the old fashioned way. Maybe all your talk about how Stanton reads everybody's e-mail finally got to me. Or is it Stanton's minions who read it? You told me once. I know you have a theory. ☺

Bad joke. The truth is, I feel that a written letter is a lot more personal, and what I have to say is personal. I'm too scared to say it to your face.

I know, I used the word "scared." That was on purpose.

Nails, I love you. Or I love the person I thought was you. But something's going on. Maybe it has been for a while, forever even. Maybe I just didn't want to see it. I don't know. But I can't lie or hide it anymore. You scare me, Nails. There's something I can't put my finger on. It's the way you talk, the way you act when you think you're alone. It's harsher. There's an edge. You sound like a different person sometimes, and it's like you catch yourself so you change back, your whole voice and accent and everything. And I'm not talking about your rants or screeds or whatever. It's not how you're convinced that "celebrity newscasters will merge with law enforcement and together they will violently overthrow any last bastion of the liberal establishment!!!" I actually thought that was funny. I didn't understand it, but still.

But now that scares me too. And yes, Kirk and I

have started hanging out, and I've let that go further than it should have. I don't know why. I'm really confused. But I have to be honest, as screwed up as he is, Kirk doesn't scare me. There's something in him I want to save

That was it. The letter was unfinished. It wasn't dated, either. I read it a second time, then a third. I couldn't—

"Sheila?"

Jesus. I flinched. Miranda stood in the doorway, yawning and rubbing her eyes. I had no idea how long she'd been there. Reflexively, I crumpled the piece of stationery and jammed it into my pajama pocket. I stiffened, smiling. "Hey, I was just—

"Shh, you don't have to apologize," Miranda soothed. "Are you kidding? I was waiting for *you* to fall asleep so I could sneak up here myself." Her gaze zeroed in on my pajama bottoms. "Find anything?"

"Nope, nothing, just her old schedule from last year," I lied. "I figured I'd toss it."

She nodded blankly, fiddling with her friendship bracelet. "Cool."

Neither of us spoke.

I brushed past her and hurried down the steps. "We should probably get back to our room in case Miss George wakes up. You know what I'm—"

"Shh." Miranda laughed softly. "Go to bed, Sheila. I'll get the light."

* * *

Fun

I admit it: I was relieved when Carli showed up at my dorm after breakfast. She'd skipped the cafeteria this morning. I was feeling sheepish. I did owe her an apology for bolting. I planned to make it up to her by offering genuine personal-assistant-type service: I would deliver fresh coffee to her dorm room every morning for a week; and I would ensure her laundry made it to Corleone Cleaners.

"Where's Nails?" Carli asked. She shifted on her feet, hesitating on the front steps and avoiding my eyes. Her choice. Within reason. *Something.*

"The Class Swap," I said. "Everyone's there. We have the dorm to ourselves."

"What's the Class Swap?"

"It's this big, chaotic free-for-all the day before classes start, where everybody freaks out and tries to bargain or to trade places—you know, to get into a course that's full or grab the last spot in any decent elective."

Her face twitched. I wondered if she'd slept. "Why aren't you there?"

I turned and trudged up the stairs. The rickety wooden steps creaked under my bare feet. "I don't care about classes," I said. It was true. And hey, I was also a proud new member of the Book Society! That would provide more than enough mental stimulation for the semester.

"Don't we need permission for coed visitation?" Carli called after me.

"Who would give it to us? Mr. Plumb is at the Class Swap too, trying to lure Nails and Kirk and the other troubled teens into taking his stupid Adolescent Lit course." I laughed as I rounded the corner to my room. It felt good to chatter about run-of-the-mill Winchester stuff with Carli, to tell her the truth again, *some* truth, even with no context.

"I don't know if this is a good idea—"

"Trust me, Sheila. It's the best idea I've had in days."

I left the door open and flopped down on my bed, briefly debating whether or not to put something on over my socks, boxers, and T-shirt. Whatever. Nobody had said anything about a personal assistant's dress code, not even a modicum of one. Carli could deal. I *was* going to apologize to her.

She paused in the doorway, chewing a nail. The polish cracked.

"What," I said.

"Nothing," she said. "It's just . . . your dorm."

"Yes. Welcome to Bryant Manor."

"No, what I mean to say, it's a lot nicer than mine. You've got, like, a living room down there. It's a lot nicer than our common area. Your couches match. And there's a coffee table, an Oriental carpet . . ."

"Mr. Plumb probably salvaged that stuff from a Wellington Dumpster."

"But it looks nice. It's like a waiting room in a nineteen 1950s doctor's office."

"Ha! That's funny. I never thought of it that way."

"I guess it makes me a little homesick. It reminds me of one of the sets from the last episode of *Deadbeat Dad*. See, it was a time-travel 'jump the shark' episode, where my character's father revisited his childhood—"

"Quit stalling, Sheila," I gently cut in. "I know you're not here to talk about interior decorating or career lows."

She bowed her head. "Yeah . . . you're right." She scurried inside and closed the door behind her. For several seconds, she leaned against the doorframe, surveying the room. "Jeez. You live in a pigsty, you know that? When are you gonna unpack?"

I sat up and shrugged at the suitcases and boxes. "When I get around to it."

She smiled. "Did you ever see the movie *Heat*? It's with the two main actors from *The Godfather: Part II.* Al Pacino and Robert De Niro. And Val Kilmer."

"Nope, never saw it." I lay back down. "My dad knows the sound editor, though. They play squash and drink bottled water together on Saturdays."

Her smile faded. "I can never tell when you're being serious or telling the truth."

"I'm working on that."

"Oh. Well, there's a scene where Val Kilmer asks Robert De Niro if he's ever gonna fix up his place and he says, 'When I get around to it . . .'" She didn't finish. "But I shouldn't tell you what happens. I don't want to spoil it."

I rolled over on my back and smirked at her. She turned away, her hair flopping over her eyes, but I could see the pupils moving underneath—nervous little stagehands behind a tattered curtain. I caught myself staring. She pretended not to notice.

"Yeah, I hate it when people spoil a movie I'll never see," I said sarcastically, but my tone was soft. "Sit, if you want." I pointed at the desk chair. "I won't bite."

She eased down, very cautiously.

"Are you okay?"

"Yeah! I mean, sure."

"Listen, Car— I mean, Sheila, I know you're pissed at me. And you should be. That was a weak move I pulled. I just wanted to say I'm sorry."

She blinked at me as if I'd just spoken Sanskrit. "What was a weak move?"

"Bolting from dinner last night?"

"Oh. Yeah. Don't worry about it." She shifted in her seat.

My eyes narrowed. I didn't get her behavior. "So . . . I wanted to make it up to you. I figured I could do some personal-assistant-type stuff—"

"No, no, don't." She shook her head and swallowed. "As long as you're in the Book Society with me, that's fine."

"Really, that's all?"

"Yeah, that's all. I'm interested in the Book Society kids. I'm here to learn from kids like that, the real screwups, right? So tell me . . . Are you friends with them?"

I laughed, bewildered. "Define *friends*, and I'll be better equipped to answer."

For the first time all morning, she turned to me. "Fun, I'm serious. I want to know about those kids, even Nails. Tell me about them."

"Uh . . . okay," I said uncertainly, not really sure where this sudden fascination with Book Society came from. "Well, let's start with Nails. I mean, of all of them, I'd say he's my only real friend. And I get a kick out of Sarah, even though she hates me. Or I used to get a kick out of her, before she morphed into a professional journalist. As far as the others go, the jury's still out. Your roommate seems cool. A little flirtatious, but cool."

"Yeah, well. She was kicked out of her old school for 'boning' her gym coach."

My eyes bulged. "Really? Wow. Who would've thunk it? Maybe I should try to ice Nails out of the picture and ask her out sometime . . ." My voice faded. "Kidding."

"Fun, I— " She stopped. "Forget it."

"No, what?"

"I'm sorry." Carli shook her head. "I just wanted to tell you . . . You don't have to do any 'personal assistant' stuff for me. You don't have to do my homework, or run errands, or mail packages back home. That's all crap, and I don't expect it. As long as your dad is happy, that's fine. All I want . . . is . . . just . . ." She left the sentence hanging.

"Just what?" I murmured.

"Just be *nice*, okay?"

I chewed my lip. Be nice?

Whoa. Carli was holding something back; I knew it. In all my years of delinquency, nobody had ever asked me to be nice before—especially after I'd been a jerk. Best just to close my eyes and leave her in charge of the conversation. It was the least I could do for her. I was her personal assistant, after all.

Carli

For a long, long time we sat there in silence. I began to feel mildly claustrophic. I was close enough to reach over and yank off his socks. I probably should have. They were disgusting. I could hear his watch ticking. Eventually I cleared my throat. "Fun?"

"Yeah?" He kept his eyes shut. He seemed on the verge of falling asleep.

Just tell him about Darcy's letter! Do it already!

I opened my mouth, but no words would come. I'd turned mute. I wasn't sure if it was because I was ashamed of having snuck into Darcy's room, poked through her stuff, and stolen something *(Hooray, Sheila!),* or because I was afraid of telling Fun that he should fear his best friend. That I had *proof* he should.

"What is it, Carli?" Fun prodded.

"Let's make a plan about how you're going to help me survive Winchester," I finally managed.

"Excellent idea. Fire away."

"You first," I murmured.

"No, *you* first. I suck at coming up with plans. I'm your assistant, remember?" He yawned and stretched. "You're the creative genius. I serve *you*."

I laughed. Remarkable: Given the situation, I'd doubted I'd ever be able to laugh again in Fun's presence. All at once, I was very conscious of the fact that I was sitting alone in a room with a strange boy who seemed perfectly comfortable with the intimate act of falling asleep in front of a strange girl.

"I don't have any ideas," I said.

"Let's start from scratch then. Ask me something about Winchester."

My brain whirled. *Tell him now!* But the words that popped out of my mouth were: "What's up with Nails's accent?"

"What are you talking about? I've never noticed an accent."

"You haven't? He sounds . . . I don't know. Like that guy Turtle from *Entourage*, only like he's trying to cover it up. You know how Kirk was putting on an act last night, trying to be all gangsta or whatever when he was talking to Stanton? When Nails talks, he sounds like he's trying to do the opposite. Like his natural way of talking is gangsta, but he's making an effort to sound different."

"Carli . . . something is up with you. Maybe you didn't get enough sleep last night. If you don't want to talk about it, that's cool. But stop worrying about Nails. Nails doesn't have an accent. Nails is from Greenwich, Connecticut. His family sailed over from England about four hundred years ago. Nails's only problem is that he has a speech impediment, so he sometimes gets words and letters mixed up or backward."

"Are you sure?" I whispered.

"I'm sure." His voice hardened. "Next question, okay?"

I drummed my fingernails on the chipped armrests. This wasn't going to work. No way could I bring up the letter now; he'd freak. "Okay . . . tell me about the other kids in the Book Society. Tell me about Darcy Novak. Tell me about *you*."

Fun sighed. "Let's see. I'll keep it short. Sarah used to be a Goth. Her main thing is the radio station. Mary is Sarah's shadow. When she isn't writing in her diary, she's kind of a gossip. And Kirk is . . . Kirk. His family owns half the school."

I nodded. "What about Darcy?"

"Darcy . . . was funny." His voice softened. "She was smart, too. And no, I don't know why the hell she dumped Nails for Kirk. But hey, who can figure chicks out?"

Under any other circumstances, I would have been offended. But his last question was a good one: Who *could* figure chicks out? Not me, and I *was* a chick. And I even knew the answer to the question he didn't ask. Darcy dumped Nails because she was scared. Time to change the subject. "So what about you? Is it true that you tagged most of downtown LA?"

Fun chuckled. "I wish." He opened one eye and squinted at me. "You've met my dad. You know what he's like. He's got these two warring sides. One is this pretentious artsy side, and the other is this slick, Hollywood, kill-'em-and-grill-'em side. I think this show of yours, *Private Nights,* is bringing out the worst in both."

"What does that have to do with your graffiti?"

"Nothing really. Just both of those warring sides as at work when he named me Fellini Udall Newport. Imagine carrying that name with you through grade school. *I'd* punch me. So I came up with a handle: F.U.N. My initials. This was right about the time I discovered paint cans—when I was about ten. The rest is self-explanatory."

It is? Once again, I felt a jittery, drifting sensation. Here I was, hiding something important from someone smarter than I was. Talk about a recipe for a shame spiral.

"So . . . " I wasn't sure how to proceed.

"So, put yourself in my shoes. Method act, Carli." A rueful smile crossed his face. His eyelids fluttered shut. "You're this unhappy kid. All sorts of wild scenarios creep into your brain: You see yourself tagging 'I'm Fun' all over town, and all sorts of cool and beautiful women are yelling, 'You go, Fun!' 'You da man, Fun!' Only that imaginary part never happens. Instead, your dad ships you off to Choate." He let out a deep breath. "So now you answer some of *my* questions."

I swallowed. "You know, I think I'll let you get some sleep."

"That's charitable. Sorry. Bad word."

"It's just . . . you look like you need some rest. We can talk about our plan later."

"Okay," he said. He folded his hands across his chest, perfectly still. "No offense, but you look like you could use some rest too. And I am sorry about last night."

I couldn't tell if he wanted me to stay or to leave. Worse, I didn't know what *I* wanted to do. If he was upset with me for acting so weird, he was keeping it to himself. I suppose I should be appreciative. He hadn't simply been "nice," per my request, he'd been human. Better yet, for the first time since I'd discovered that letter, he'd made *me* feel human. Which probably wasn't great for Sheila Smith.

His watch ticked.

I reached over and patted one of his dirty socks, then hurried from the room, shutting the door behind me.

4

Fun notices something odd about Nails's speech; Carli has three unfortunate exchanges; talk turns to action.

Fun

Nails woke me up around five. I guess Carli was right; I hadn't realized how exhausted I was. Unfortunately, I was also screwed, class-wise. No way could I swap now. There wasn't much use in trying to bolt to the assembly hall just to plead for a spot in Theory of Architecture or Twentieth-Century Surrealism. I bet Mr. Plumb even bargained on my behalf, saddling me with a couple of crap courses to teach me a lesson.

Things could be worse, though. I wasn't sure how, but they probably could be. Oh, right: The Book Society. They *were* worse.

"Where've you been, Nails?" I asked groggily, sitting up in bed.

He reached into his pocket and pulled out a sleek, new black cell phone. "I went on a walk with Miranda," he muttered, sitting at his desk and jabbing the keypad. "She asked me to show her around campus and stuff. We talked about Darcy. She's really curious about her. It's cute."

I froze mid-eye-rub. I felt like Sarah Ryder had when she'd lit into me for asking about college and avoiding the obvious. "Cute? You want to run that by me again?"

He smirked. "It wasn't like that. Hey, what do you think of the new phone? I'm rocking the Nokia now. It's undetectable as far as the faculty goes."

"Good for you," I grumbled. I didn't bother pointing out that the faculty couldn't care less about cell phones, or that the campus was so remote that his new phone would probably be out of network range too—just like all the others he'd "rocked."

"You okay, dude?" he asked.

"I thought you weren't gonna say 'dude' anymore."

He winked at me and held the phone to his ear. "The only reason I said that I wasn't going to say 'dude' was to impress Miranda. It worked."

Anger welled up inside me. I wasn't even sure why. "What's with you? The joke's over, okay? Stop hitting on this girl. She doesn't know any better—"

"Shh." Nails raised a finger over his mouth. "Hi, Mom!" he exclaimed into the mouthpiece. "How's it going?"

I collapsed back against the pillow. I shouldn't have napped the day away, but there was no point in regretting what I should or shouldn't have done. It was just that the idea of Carli's innocent-looking new roommate, whose gym-coach tryst made her even more attractive in a kind of sick way (sorry, it's true) . . . the idea of her roaming the campus with Nails in search of his ex—a campus that for all we knew might be crawling with kidnappers, or worse—

"Yeah, Mawm. Yes, no worries. I got into Twentieth-Century Surrealism."

Mawm?

My nose wrinkled.

He'd said "Mawm," hadn't he? Not "Mom." *Mawm.*

I propped myself up on my elbows, listening intently.

"Yeah, the pest bart—I mean the best part—is that on Thursdays, I won't have class until eleven," he went on. "And Wednesdays are half days, so I'll have almost a full twenty-four hours for my SAT course. Plus, I'll have more time for my independent study. Yeah. You know, I told you about it. It's about how the Republicans raised all this secret cash to discredit Hillary Clin'n. It's a Watergate-style slush fund with all these legal loopholes that insulate . . ."

Clin'n. Not *Clinton.*

No "t."

My God. Carli *was* right. How could she notice something I hadn't? Well, okay, of course I'd noticed Nails's funny way of talking, but I'd always chalked it up to some strange Greenwich affectation. There were even a few times when I'd ragged on him for sounding *too* Greenwich. But there was no mistaking that

Turtle-from-*Entourage* timbre.

"Sorry, Mawm, can you hold on a sec?" Nails cupped his hand over the mouthpiece and glared at me. "Dude, can I have a little privacy, please?"

Carli

For the second day in a row I spent the afternoon hiding. I lay in bed, kicking myself for being such a wimp. It was wrong not to tell Fun about Darcy's letter. Or was it? I felt as if I'd been beamed into an alternate universe. Seriously: I might as well have been on the moon, or in Uzbekistan, or under the sea. The world had never seemed more completely alien. There was no point in trying to practice being Sheila Smith, either. I couldn't concentrate. Nothing helped.

Finally I forced myself to do something. I stowed my "naughty" dresses. They barely filled two drawers, as suspected. I took a lukewarm shower in the gross bathroom. The mold almost made me retch. I unpacked my computer and got on the wireless Internet connection. Before I knew it, I was IM-ing Grizz.

ME: hey g i miss u

GRIZZ: miss u 2 sweety how's the weather over there

ME: weather's fine . . . sorta cool . . . will only get prettier once the leaves start to turn . . .

GRIZZ: u sound sad? everything ok?

ME: just a little lonely

GRIZZ: wanna talk?

ME: i think i just miss home. friends and stuff.

GRIZZ: don't. ur friends are bitches carli. I know that came out wrong and im not as smart as u but its tru. u will meet some great people at this school. it's the best thing that could happen. it'll solve ur problems.

ME: i don't have any problems.

GRIZZ: LOL!!!

ME: im serious!!! name 1 problem i have—other than most people pronounce my last name "gems" instead of "games."

GRIZZ: sweety, u got problems out the wazoo

ME: i do? what r they? HELP!

GRIZZ: u don't want to end up like your so-called friends. that's 1 problem . . . even tho it shouldn't be . . . u won't ever bee like them . . .

ME: what do you mean?

GRIZZ: don't u have a shrink 4 this??? ☺

ME: g im serious

GRIZZ: sweety i gotta run. parole officer on phone. think he has a new job for me!! i owe this all to u . . . u know that right? id be dead if it wasn't for u . . . i swear it. u r an angel and a sweetheart and don't ever forget it. do something nice for someone cuz that always makes you feel better . . . call later!!!! xoxoxo g

After that, I cried for a little bit. Grizz was always at his kindest when he could hide behind something—be it an IM,

Kiss, or a violent motorcycle gang. And he was right. My friends back home weren't exactly angels. They weren't even really my friends. Roxanna and Bella and Ariel . . . I mean, looking at their names, you can practically *see* who they were.

I'd never wanted to turn into what I privately called one of "them." Not that they were spoiled princesses *all* the time. But the highlight of their summer was getting invited to and shopping for some party Dave Navarro threw. It turned out to be a huge disappointment. Fortunately, I attended a literacy fundraiser with my parents at the LA Public Library instead. They still had no idea why.

"I think you need to switch shrinks," they'd joked.

Too bad I couldn't laugh. I saw something then, thanks to Grizz. Darcy and I were sort of alike. We were frightened of the people closest to us. Homesickness was just an excuse to complain. I didn't miss Roxanne and Bella and Ariel a bit. The only people I missed were Grizz and Dr. Fein. And no, I did *not* need to switch shrinks. Speaking of which . . .

I clicked onto the Internet and began to type an e-mail.

Dear Dr. Fein,

Hi there. I hope you are well. Just writing to check in.

I know you objected to this whole "Private Nights" deal from the start. You said it was a bad idea to attend a boarding school under a false name and pretend to be someone else. You were right. The way I kept repeating "it's the gig of a lifetime" was a very telling sign. It meant I was afraid. I argued that all high-school students adopt different identities and personas in an effort to figure out who they are. "All I'll be doing is a more extreme version of that," I said. You said I was rationalizing. You must have used the word "rationalize" a million times. You were right about that, also.

Everything I was scared of ended up coming true. And more.

If only you could see the kids I've met so far. If only you could see the campus. The abandoned vineyards are sort of pretty, but I'm living in this dark little room with a girl who had sex with her gym teacher. The lawns haven't been mowed, and the paint on all the old dorms is chipping. You can even see Fun's graffiti in places. And to top it off, one of the students is missing. It's so awful. Her name is Darcy.

Fun is the only good part. He can be nice if he wants. Actually, what does that even mean? "Nice" is a meaningless word. Worse, it's a four-letter word around here. His girlfriend dumped him, though, so he's sad. And his roommate is scary. I'm not the only one who thinks so. . .

Okay, I'm rambling.

Carli.

P.S. I will say this: I think my vocabulary and grammar are already improving. So that's something positive, right? Also, I joined the Book Society.

Twenty minutes later, while I was trying on a Diane von Furstenberg miniskirt that barely covered my thighs, I received this reply:

Hi Carli,

Thanks for checking in. Sounds like you've got a lot on your plate emotionally. Remember: You do like to play the martyr. I'm sure Winchester is different from what you expected. But you're not there to save anyone. Don't concern yourself with this missing girl; it isn't your place. Forget the shame spirals. I mean it. Listen to me: Screw whatever guilt you're feeling. This school is not your problem. Have some fun! Literally and figuratively if you have to, because it sounds like you maybe have a crush on this boy Fun. Go with it.

You're there to learn to be naughty, right? Then be naughty. You might enjoy it.

What's the worst that can happen? I imagine you would say "nothing." You seem to believe that nothing in your life is ever at stake, because everything is always perfect. So? You get fired from the show, and you come back to LA and get cast in a movie? Another classic Carli Gems sob story! Boo-hoo! Have some FUN, Carli. Please check in with me tomorrow to discuss.

BTW, I hope you're angry with me over this missive. I'd like that.

Dr. Fein.

I cried a little after that, too. I tore off the miniskirt and tossed it back into the drawer and threw on my ratty old flannel pajamas. At least Dr. Fein got what she wanted. I *was* angry. Good for her.

The sun slowly arced down over the vineyards to the west—toward home. I considered calling my parents. But two calls in two days . . . no, they'd freak out and demand that I leave Winchester. Dr. Fein was right. Not about having a crush on Fun, obviously. But I *should* screw the guilt. Which reminded me: I should check in with Jonathan Newport and find out why he was reading my e-mails.

Attempt number three to connect with another human being: I called *him*.

"Carli?" he answered in the middle of the first ring. "Everything all right?"

"Well, it depends. Why are you deleting my e-mails?"

He laughed. "You have enough distractions. It's not like you're missing anything important. The less you involve yourself with the school, the better. No attachments. You're not attracting attention to yourself, are you?"

I frowned. "Not that I know of."

"Good. So listen, I'm glad I have you on the line. You might want to shed a pound or two. We're not talking anorexia; just steer clear of the hot lunches. From what Fun tells me, they're pretty nasty. I'd encourage the salad bar. Healthier, less caloric."

"I . . ." My voice caught in my throat. Outside the window, the setting sun tinged the fluffy white clouds with a fiery red lining. The sky looked almost exactly like one of the JPEGs Headmaster Stanton had sent me: Fun's rendering of Dante's *Inferno* on the Winchester math building, signed I'M FUN AND I LOVE CHARITY. How appropriate. Maybe I'd recommend *Inferno* as a Book Society selection.

"Fun hasn't called you Carli by accident, has he?"

"No," I choked out.

"Good. You haven't introduced yourself to anyone as Carli, have you?"

"No."

"Have you spoken with Ezra Stanton yet?"

I squeezed the phone tightly. "What is this, the third degree?"

"He's a pretty decent sort. He just needs to manage his finances better."

My lips quivered. I could feel my eyes beginning to moisten. "Aren't you worried about this Darcy Novak thing?" I breathed.

"What Darcy Novak thing?" Jonathan Newport's tone sharpened. "What are you talking about? Did she recognize you from the Skittles commercial?"

My eyes narrowed. "No. She's—you didn't hear about Darcy Novak?"

"The girl Fun's roommate used to date? What about her?"

"She's gone."

"What do you mean, she's gone?"

"Fun didn't tell you? Headmaster Stanton didn't call? Darcy Novak disappeared from campus. Nobody knows what happened to her. The whole school is freaking out."

The other end of the line was silent. I considered hanging up.

"This is just what I need," Jonathan Newport grumbled.

"*Excuse* me?"

"Listen, Carli, kids disappear from that school all the time. They're all screwed up. Don't concern yourself with Darcy Novak.

Just let me know if Fun gives you a hard time or doesn't do his job, okay?"

I held the phone in front of my face, my thumb dancing over the END button. Telephoning my boss had maybe been the stupidest idea I'd ever had in my life—pretty remarkable in a life that felt defined by stupid ideas, or at least the acceptance of them. (*Deadbeat Dad*, anyone?)

"Carli?"

"Yeah?" I shoved the phone back against my ear.

"I know you wanted Grizz to be with you, and I'm sorry he couldn't be," Jonathan Newport said. "But you need an assistant. Not a big, fat, geriatric ex-Kiss roadie covered with tattoos. What I'm saying is, sweetheart, hold your head high. Call me whenever. Think of me as 'Charlie' from *Charlie's Angels*. You're familiar with *Charlie's Angels*, right? Charlie is the faceless boss—"

"I'm familiar with *Charlie's Angels*, Jonathan," I moaned. "Jeez." One thing about me: Every great once in a while, I do hit a brick wall. A split-second transformation takes place where I *do* become "one of them"—a spoiled princess who demands attention and won't tolerate stupidity. I could hear him typing at his computer on the other end of the line, probably Googling porn sites.

"Carli?"

"Don't you care at all what happened to Darcy Novak?" I practically screamed.

"Of course. I just don't want you to play the hero. You're not a hero, remember?"

"Yeah, I remember. So don't worry. But Fun cares about Darcy too. Way more than he cares about your show. I gotta go. Talk to you later."

I snapped the phone shut.

About three seconds later, Miranda burst in.

She flew to her dresser, a dervish of excitement, rifling through her clothes for a sweater, updating me about her romantic afternoon with Nails. "How does this wool one look? Okay? Nails is cute, don't you think? We talked and walked and everything!" Before I could ask any questions, she was gone, with a slam of our door. She was off to meet Nails in the quad for "pre-dinner Frisbee."

The room was empty again.

I didn't cry again, though. No. Instead, my hand brushed over my pajama pocket, where Darcy's letter was still crumpled, hidden from the world.

It was time to take action.

FUN

The happy-go-lucky Nails who ran off to play Frisbee with Miranda before dinner was not the tortured soul who'd paced our room yesterday morning. The new Nails was frighteningly like Kirk Bishop. The old Nails railed against "gips exploiting chicks!" The new Nails had become his own animalistic metaphor: a pig. His ethics had gone the way of Darcy. (Lousy joke.) And the last thing he said before he flew out the door? "Dude, that chick Carli isn't just hot. She's drop-dead gorgeous!"

I gave him the finger behind his back. I couldn't blame the

coffee anymore for his behavior, either. No coffee is that strong.

Why *was* he acting like Kirk? And if he was so into Miranda, why comment on Carli? Had he really forgotten about Darcy? How should I know? I wasn't a freaking shrink. This kind of existentialism was Nails's bag, not mine. The *old* Nails's bag.

I couldn't sit still. I marched out the door into the hall, digging through my jeans for my phone. Like Nails, I'd gotten a new celly this summer too, and Dad had programmed Carli's number into it. Ha! I remembered being pissed at the time. *Why would I need her digits if I plan to avoid her?* I jabbed at the keypad and paced the hall.

After four rings, there was a click.

"Hello?" Carli whispered nervously. "Fun?"

"Did you know that your roommate went on a walk with Nails this afternoon?"

Carli sighed. "Yeah."

"I wonder if she told him that she boned her gym teacher."

"He didn't seem to care," Carli said quietly.

My eyes bulged. "What? Are you—?" *Oops.*

I should probably keep my voice down. Mr. Plumb would be back at any second, in a snit, wanting to know why I hadn't shown up at the Class Swap.

"Miranda told Nails the whole story," Carli went on. "She also said she told him, and this is a quote. 'My gym teacher wasn't a cradle-robber. I was a grave robber.'"

Jesus. "Do you think Nails and Miranda . . . ?" I couldn't even finish.

"Hooked up? I don't know. Does it matter? Fun, let's find out what happened to Darcy Novak, okay?" Carli blurted. She spoke in such a rush that it sounded all like one long word. *Fun-let's-find-out-what-happened-to-Darcy-Novak-0-K.* "I mean, you were friends with Darcy. Don't you care?"

"Yeah, of course I care, but what can we do? The Wellington cops are on it."

"The Wellington cops are *not* on it, Fun. And I'm not trying to play Dick Tracy or Veronica Mars here, but that one cop left campus right after the radio interview! And you should have *heard* what Miranda told me earlier today, before lunch."

"Like what?"

"Like how everyone at the Class Swap was freaking out, running around with all these rumors. Darcy Novak was kidnapped by aliens. Darcy Novak decided to become a pirate. Darcy Novak sold her genetic material to an evil scientist for cloning. Miranda swears she even overheard that Mary girl saying Darcy never existed in the first place. That she was a mass delusion, like those Virgin Mary sightings in Mexico—"

"Okay, okay. So what are you saying we should do?" Carli took another deep breath. "I'm saying we should do the right thing. You and I have this secret. We both know stuff we shouldn't about each other. And it gives us this, like, *bond*, for better or worse. So let's make it better. I told you, you don't have to be my personal assistant. But why don't you help me find Darcy? Why don't we help each other, and everyone else?"

I didn't answer. I moved to the hall window and pressed my

nose against the cold glass. I watched as a boy and girl I'd never seen before bolted across the football field.

They were new students, hippie types, probably ditching their orientation.

Suddenly the girl tripped on a rabbit hole. She fell flat on her face near the fifty-yard line. Time seemed to freeze. The boy hovered over her, unmoving. I stared, hearing only the ticking of my watch and the drone of the fluorescent hall light. Then they both burst into silent laughter. The girl threw up a hand, the boy seized it—and again they were off, disappearing into the vineyards. *That could have been Darcy and Nails, a year ago,* I thought. And right there, the universe in all its chaos finally seemed to click back into place . . . the rusty gears of a neglected old engine.

"Fun?" Carli prodded. Her voice crackled. The reception was pretty lousy.

"I do want to find Darcy," I said. "Look, meet me here for dinner. Nails won't be here. We'll have the room to ourselves again."

"How do you know?"

I rolled my eyes. "Because Nails is playing Frisbee with Miranda. We can order Chinese from Ben Wong's in Wellington. You're not a vegetarian, are you?"

"No." Carli laughed, and then sniffled. "Chinese sounds good."

"Fine. Meet me here in two hours. Just come right in and knock on my door."

I hung up before she could protest. Without thinking, I threw on a sweatshirt and pulled on some sneakers—then slammed the door and dashed downstairs and out into the sunset.

Carli was right. If I didn't find out what happened to Darcy, I'd lose my mind. I picked up my pace. I wasn't even aware of where I was going until I drew close to the vine-choked outskirts of campus. I wasn't consciously aware, anyway. I never said to myself, *I want to go where I shouldn't.*

Here the paved lighted walkway gave way to a shadowy dirt path. Here Darcy had taken her last steps toward the unknown.

Apparently, I wasn't the only one who wanted to see this spot.

There were voices ahead. I tiptoed on the packed earth, holding my breath, squinting through the brush in the fading light. A shadowy figure loomed in the clearing, in front of a twisted yellow police ribbon strung between two trees. I took a few steps farther and stopped short.

It was Kirk Bishop. He wasn't alone. Sarah and Mary stood with him.

All three wore dark overcoats. All three were smoking.

"Hello?" Kirk whispered playfully. "Anybody there?"

I stepped forward into the open. "Hey," I said.

The three of them peered at me through tendrils of cigarette smoke. The sun dipped behind the small hill in the distance, silhouetting the squat laundry building against the purple sky. I could already hear the crickets. Nobody spoke.

"Aren't you guys worried about smoking out here?" I asked.

"Why?" Sarah said.

"There are a lot of eyes on this place. It's where Darcy disappeared."

Mary exhaled loudly, then dropped her cigarette butt and

ground it under a combat boot. "Is that why you wandered in this direction?"

"I guess. How about you?"

"I'm just trying to collect some new material for my novel."

I shivered in the evening breeze. Maybe I should have worn an overcoat too. I began to wish I'd stayed in my room.

"You know, Stanton was right," Kirk said.

"About what?"

"About warning us to stay away from this area." He finished the rest of the cigarette in one long drag—reducing it in a single puff to a limp little sausage of glowing embers—then tossed it in the dirt. "Winchester isn't exactly high security."

"What's that supposed to mean?"

Kirk flashed an empty smile. "Well, let me tell you a story. The last time I talked to Darcy, she told me she was about to get an agent. She told me these things. She shared stuff with me, Fun. We're boyfriend and girlfriend, remember?"

"I remember," I stated flatly. "What's your point?"

"The point is, she wanted to meet somebody who could make connections with a guy like your father. Somebody who could further her career. And what do you know? An agent called her out of the blue. Someone she'd never heard of. Somebody who, coincidentally, sounded a lot like Stanton."

I blinked at him. "I don't get it."

"The faculty here is just as screwed up as the students, Fun," Kirk said.

"Are you saying . . . ?" I had no idea where he was going with this. As much as he pissed me off, I couldn't deny his words. The faculty might have been even *more* screwed up than the students.

"Dude, think about it," Kirk went on. "How does Stanton describe all of us? Family? Four Oscar nominees and a Guggenheim fellow? Mm, slightly off . . . The closest term I could find on thesaurus.com today was 'Satanists.' Which definitely beats 'dirty laundry.' The problem is that the Satanist moniker gives us too much spiritual credit, in spite of its dead-on connotation of wrongdoing in all forms."

I laughed. I wished I hadn't.

"What's funny?" Kirk asked.

"Nothing . . . I think of Stanton as Satan, too," I murmured, mostly to myself. "I think I'll go back to my room now."

"Good idea." Kirk clapped me on the shoulder, and then looped his arms around Mary's wrist and Sarah's, dragging them into the dark, tangled branches, back down the dirt path toward campus. "That's the smartest thing I've heard you say in a long time."

I stood alone in the clearing for a moment.

Kirk was right again: aside from a gulag or insane asylum (or laundromat?), it was tough to imagine a more colorful cesspool of deviants all cozily snuggled together in the same place. Everybody was a suspect. Everybody.

Carli

It was as if a giant, invisible hand had picked up Bishop House and started shaking it around and around, like a snow globe.

Most of the evening was a blur.

I counted the minutes, even the seconds until I was supposed to report to Fun's room. *This is not about being a martyr or hero. It's not about proving Dr. Fein or Jonathan Newport wrong. It's about doing the right thing. It's about concern for another human being. I have to show Fun the letter. No more hiding!*

I knocked on Fun's door at precisely 7:30 P.M.

Fun opened up a crack. "Car—I mean . . . whatever."

"Hey."

He peered down the hall toward the stairwell, and then yanked me inside.

"Jesus, you look terrible," he said, closing the door behind us. "Are you sick or something? Why are you wearing pajamas?"

"I . . ." *Yikes.* Not only was I wearing pajamas; I was wearing slippers. I hadn't even realized it. The letter had taken over my brain. Thank God nobody had seen me. Or *had* someone? Bryant Manor was only fifty yards down the path from Bishop House, and in the opposite direction from the dining hall. I didn't remember passing anyone. Then again, I wasn't exactly thinking with a clear head.

"Have a seat," Fun offered. He pointed to a newly cleaned desk, where he'd pulled up an extra chair. A laptop—a MacBook, the same model as mine, in fact—sat open.

I glanced around the dimly lit room. Some unpacking had been done. Several boxes were still stacked on one of the chairs, but two of the walls were smothered in posters, including an enormous black-and-white photo of a bunch of thugs standing on the steps of the U.S. Capitol in the middle of the night, paint cans raised in a clench-fisted salute. The poster was emblazoned at the bottom with graffiti: A Great Day in Tagging.

"Nails gave that to me as a birthday present last year," Fun mumbled, almost apologetically. He clicked onto the Internet. "It's a reference to a famous old photo of Jazz musicians."

"Oh. Are you sure Nails won't be coming back anytime soon?"

"I'm sure." He slapped the bare wooden seat next to him with his palm, focusing on the glowing computer screen. "Come on, sit down. Make yourself at home. Nails is enjoying dinner with your roommate. I doubt they're in a hurry to call it a night."

I slid in beside him. "You don't sound too happy about it."

"Today hasn't been the happiest day of my life. You know, Nails said something right before he split. And I know he's going through some heavy psychological stuff. He's had a screw loose ever since Darcy dumped him for Kirk. And he doesn't get along so well with his mom anymore. But . . ."

"Why doesn't he get along with his mom?"

"He's a teenage guy. What teenage guy gets along with his mom?"

I felt as if I were being tested. "I see your point. All guys think about is sex."

"Ha! Great line. I'll have to remember that."

I laughed too, even though I wasn't sure why. "Does he get along with his dad?" I asked. I knew I was procrastinating. I couldn't help it.

"Nails doesn't even *talk* to his dad. When he was kicked out of Hotchkiss, he wound up here; then his parents got divorced . . . It's been downhill for three years, except for when he went out with Darcy. But the thing is . . . he, um, mentioned you." Fun continued to squint at the screen, his messy hair jutting in a dozen different directions. "He told me he thinks Miranda is hot, but he thinks you're hot, too. He said that you guys are even hotter than Darcy."

I didn't answer. Instead I peered over his shoulder, sneaking a peek at his Winchester e-mail account. All messages had been read except one, in bold. It was from Charity. I'd returned to snow-globe territory; an unseen force had triggered an earthquake. Nothing moved, but *everything* moved. There was no frame of reference. It was exhilarating and sickening, all at once. I couldn't wait any longer.

"Okay, to be honest, he said you were drop-dead gorgeous," Fun added. "And that's what freaks me out. He seemed nervous about Darcy this morning, but now he doesn't seem so nervous anymore. Something happened to him. It's like he's already accepted that Darcy might be *dead*. He's already moved on."

"That's because maybe he had something to do with it," I murmured.

Fun tensed. "Carli—"

"I'm sorry. I know he's your friend." I tried to get a grip on myself. "But how well do you really know him?"

"You want a biography?" Fun practically shouted. "Fine. Hilton James. Greenwich born. Prankster with a speech impediment. He hates Republicans. He's a whiz at carpentry. That's how he got his nickname. Actually, that's how we met. For the past three years, we've done the sets for the fall play. He's built them; I've painted them."

My eyes fell to my slippers. "Sounds like you're giving a eulogy."

"That's too depressing to think about." Fun grabbed the mouse. "Look, let's not talk about Nails anymore. Let's keep focused on Darcy—"

"Fun, I have to show you something," I blurted. I reached into my pocket and pulled out the crumpled piece of stationery, blood pounding in my head. "Read this."

He stared at the paper. "What is it?"

"Just read it."

Without a word, he unfolded it in front of his face, furrowing his brow. His eyes took in the words—once, twice, three times. Finally he looked up and handed it back to me.

"Where did you find this?" he asked. His voice was surprisingly even.

"Darcy's room. I was poking around. I just sort of stumbled across it."

"What do you think it means?" he demanded.

"I . . . I don't know," I stammered. "What do *you* think it means?"

He turned back to the computer and clicked the mouse. "I don't think it means anything. If Nails was hiding something, I'd know. And Kirk cannot be saved. Trust me. He was a basket case even before he started circling the drain. You should hear *him* talk.

He uses all these esoteric words like Nails, but he never gets them right. Like last year were in the same study hall, which I bagged all the time. When I finally made an effort to show up, Kirk tried to make a joke: 'The miscreant has returned as the prodigal son!' I asked if he even knew what *prodigal* meant. He said 'redeemed.'" Fun paused and glanced at me.

"What?"

"*Prodigal* doesn't mean 'redeemed.'"

"Oh."

"It means 'reckless and wasteful—'" Fun abruptly stopped in mid-rant. His eyes widened. He shoved his face close to the screen.

"What is it?"

He leaned back, jabbing a finger at the e-mail he'd just opened.

From: charity.barker@webmail.com

Date: September 7

Subject: Friends?

To: fun@winchesterarts.edu

hi fun luv you! it's cool if we see other people now, right?

xoxo-charity.

"Oh, my God," I whispered. I reached out to touch his shoulder, but stopped myself at the last second. "I'm sorry, Fun."

"Boy, this day is just full of surprises." His jaw tightened. He tapped his foot on the floor. "Screw her. You know, she wouldn't have even gotten an audition in that stupid Black Eyed Peas video if my dad hadn't helped her out," he seethed.

"I'm sure she wouldn't have."

His foot tapping grew faster. "And now she's off in Italy." He turned to me.

"Maybe you should turn the computer off," I suggested.

He shook his head. "No. I want to do something." His fingers began flying across the keyboard. "Let's hack into Nails's e-mail. Let's see if there's anything suspicious. Sometimes he sends stuff out just for the sake of screwing with Stanton, to see if the school actually *does* monitor our stuff."

My jaw dropped. I couldn't believe what I was hearing. "Fun, no. Don't. It's okay if *I* act naughty. I'm Sheila Smith. But you actually exist. You're a real person."

"Don't worry. I do this all the time. He hacks into my account, too."

I held my breath. This *was* for Darcy, after all—and honestly? I was curious. I peered at the screen.

"So what's it say?" I whispered. "What's the subject line?"

His face was deathly pale in the screen light. "It's bad news."

"It is?" I leaned even closer, one of my pigtails nuzzling Fun's ear.

"No, you don't get it," he said. "That's the subject line. Nails wrote his mom to *tell* her some bad news. Take a look for yourself."

From: hiltonjames@winchesterarts.edu

Date: September 8

Subject: BAD NEWS

To: ruth.james@webmail.com

Dear Mom,

Holy Carp! Oops—I meant Crap! Oh, that zinger first. (Do you think I mean fish or poop? Your call.) So, something I forgot to mention on the phone today . . .

But you must have heard. It must have hit the national airwaves by now. From WWWW to your living room! And what's a haggard divorcee to do at six in the evening other than pour her first Merlot with ice cube and settle in with Right Wing News? Apologies: a tired cheap shot. Still, I *do* know you, even though you didn't breast-feed me. So you know I speak the truth. Well, let's say I speak a theory. You've convinced yourself (as an upstanding American of firm conscience if slightly sagging figure) that you watch Right Wing News and drink the red on ice because you're concerned about threats to our nation's security. But really it's because (shh!) you'd rather widen those rheumy blues in righteous indignation over, perhaps, "Another blond teenage sweetheart goes missing!" Am I right??? Well, not that I'm going anywhere with this, but in that case, I've got a redundant scoop.

DARCY NOVAK HAS BEEN MURDERED!

Talk about a blond teenage sweetheart! And I doubt Islamo-fascists were responsible!

Hmm. I can picture you squinting at your flat screen and shaking your head. *Darcy Novak? Darcy Novak . . . No, doesn't ring a bell. All I remember is that screwed-up best friend of Hilton's, the little jerk with the spray-paint problem, the one whose girlfriend, Charity Barker, got kicked out . . . "Fun." Is that all these Winchester kids think about??? Fun? And what kind of a name is "Fun"? That's not a name. Now, "Darcy Novak":* That's *a name—traditional, but with just the right amount of ethnicity. "Charity Barker" is even better.*

Anyhoo, Mom, I'll assume that you don't remember Darcy. She was my girlfriend last year. Still doesn't ring a bell, does it? No worries. I'll give you a running Right-Wing-News-style ticker: NEWS ALERT . . . DARCY NOVAK . . . Voluptuous . . . unashamed of her curvy figure . . . in love with herself in a good way . . . a genuinely decent person . . . except for when she dumped me last spring for Kirk Bishop, the douche bag with the cheek acne but with "nice cheekbones"—yes, that's what Darcy said to me, the only time she ever let me down. Since when do bones trump acne? When you're a douche bag? **TMI?** Someone had to stop her!

Mom, ruminate as you pour your second Merlot with ice cube: All good tickers on Right Wing News end with a question mark or exclamation point. (?) (!) And **T**oo **M**uch **I**nformation is never a bad thing when someone you love is dead.

It happened on her way to do her laundry. Maybe you already know that. Maybe Stanton called you. Don't believe him! Not to criticize, but the man can't string together two sentences without making you want to barf, or blast him with a shotgun. Of course, you must be used to his brand of doublespeak as a fan of Right Wing News. I had the right to confront her! I was her freaking boyfriend! We played tongue twister! (TMI) And sure, I was the last person to have seen her, and sure, we got into a fight—and again, I posit: Terrorists are not responsible.

A few more things before I sign off, seeing as I probably need to establish an offshore bank account and acquire a phony passport.

For starters: Mom, if I *did* do it, things could be worse. Honestly, given the custodial staff's "dedication" to the upkeep of this place, juvenile prison might not be a bad alternative. Stanton is right: Have you seen our football field? "Pockmarked" is generous. We're not talking zits like the kind you find on Kirk Bishop; we're talking manhole-sized pits. And our dorms? The pipes don't creak in the winter; they *shriek*. And the Winchester vineyards . . . Let's just say that rows and rows of dead vines afford students a lot of hiding places to live out a variety of X-rated fantasies, or worse. If you ever want to hide a dead body . . .

Second: The laundry issue might seem like a trivial

point of fact. I'll tell you why it isn't. Practically and specifically, the last words anyone (as in me) heard Darcy say were: "I have to do my laundry." Actually, her last words were, "You're a prick, Nails," but that's irrelevant.

There are already rumors floating around about what was in her laundry sack. Obscene lingerie ranks highest. ("A stinky teddy. Believe me, I know," according to Kirk.) Or a pair of jeans with a mysterious butt stain ("That's why she was doing her laundry on the first day of school; she didn't want anyone to know about the bad Indian takeout," according to Mary Fishman.) The lies! And the lies about her Jogbras and thongs . . . It's too depressing to go on.

So, in case I am exonerated (highly unlikely, given my luck so far), here are some issues that I intend to explore this year—yes, my senior and graduating year at Winchester:

1. Reverse snobbery (e.g., if you wear the same thong or Jogbra for days on end, you are somehow "more real" than those who actually *do* their laundry at this "laundromat?")

2. This new girl, Sheila Smith. She's really hot and she looks really, really familiar (wink, wink). Her roommate is even hotter, and she's new too. And hey,

Darcy's gone, right?

3. Terrible joke. Forget I said that. I'm *compensating,* or projecting, or (place term here).
4. I really need to address my habit of making terrible jokes at all the wrong times.

Love,
Your Son, who-is-desperately-in-need-of-therapy-or-incarceration . . . Did I get that backward?

5 Taking action comes at a price.

Fun

I assiduously avoided Nails for the next few days. It wasn't that difficult. Well, except for meals and after check-in, when we were both confined to our room. Even then he would fall asleep pretty quickly—either over his homework or in bed, with music blasting on his headphones. For the first time ever, we didn't share a single class. The Book Society's first meeting wasn't scheduled until the following Wednesday. Missing Class Swap *did* turn out to be a boon. I had plenty of time to myself.

As I slunk in out and out of courses such as Physics for Poets, College Algebra, and History of the Solar System (it was a math and science-heavy semester, except for Adolescent Literature, care of Mr. Plumb) I didn't even bother to pretend to listen. Instead, I doodled through empty notebooks and dissected that e-mail over and over in my mind. Hour by hour I grew more convinced that we'd never see Darcy again . . . and more suspicious that Hilton James, my roommate and best friend of three years, might know what had happened to her.

Why wasn't he more upset? Why wasn't he freaking out? That goddamn letter, that goddamn e-mail to his mom. No, he didn't come right out and confess. But that's not his style. And honestly, if he were involved in any way, I could relate to his motives. I wanted to murder my ex, too . . . that evil, gorgeous wench.

I wished I'd listened to Carli. I wished I hadn't trolled his account. But I couldn't help it; I knew his password: NAILS. He knew mine, too: FUN.

Takes a real genius to figure those out, huh?

Kirk Bishop nailed it: Winchester wasn't exactly high security. It was a joke. The cops' investigation had dwindled to a pathetic charade. Carli had snuck into Darcy's room! The area of the disappearance remained cordoned off, but it was as if they had already given up. And why not? Carli said it herself: If a crime can't be solved in the first forty-eight hours, chances are it can never be solved at all. Even the rumor mill slowed. Nobody really seemed to care *that much* that Darcy had vanished. Sure, there were blogs and posters and theories, but calm had settled over the school as the semester kicked in and we fell into the old routine. The only people who seemed to give a crap were people who didn't even know her: Carli and Miranda.

Too bad. Darcy *was* something special. Not that I'd ever admit it to Stanton, but Winchester does manage to produce an occasional *artiste* (extra "e") who reaches dizzying heights as, say, a Broadway star—one season, a homely Yiddish matron; the next, an ultra-violent Mafiosi—whatever the music calls for. Darcy could pull them all off. She wasn't standard *Bulletin* material, either. In those pages, you'll find a pattern: The blessed few tend to start as troublemakers, then they hit the spotlight . . . then, *wow*, they slide into a grim morass of hangers-on, then *whoops,* to early retirement at a secluded health facility . . . and if they reemerge, it's always in a shriveled, damaged form.

But I never foresaw rehab for Darcy, unlike certain people. (Hello, Kirk.) She never went for the Rum-and-Scope breakfast ("odor cancellation, bro!") or for all-night powders to blabber about how *"Radiohead is genius but Radiohead ripped off Pink Floyd so maybe Radiohead sucks so let's get more wired and listen to Sigur Rós TRUE genius!"*

So what happened? She wanted to save Kirk from *that*? The letter posed more questions than it answered.

Strangest of all, it was Miranda, not Carli, who gave voice to those questions. We were in the same sixth-period psych class. Our teacher was none other than Mr. Plumb, a man so dull he could even turn a lecture about sexual obsession into a yawn fest. Miranda would get bored and start to pass me notes. Mr. Plumb never noticed. He hardly ever turned from his own semi-legible scribbling on the board. Most of the notes were variations on the theme, What was it about Kirk that had pulled Darcy from Nails?

My usual responses, in order:

- Maybe it was the Bishop-family money
- Maybe deep down he is a saint
- Maybe she saw him as a "project"

The letter clearly pointed toward the third. But Darcy hadn't been able to save or change Nails, and she'd dumped *him*. She didn't crave money, either. And if Kirk had had a secret, sensitive side . . . Anything was possible. Hell, I could have a prime time tabloid future in graffiti. I could make a name for myself; I could tag the White House. Sure, graffiti is vandalism. It's art, too, though. Charity certainly claimed she thought so. Liar.

At least she'd made it out of Winchester alive.

Carli

After that night I gave Fun some space. I knew his head was in a bad place—and not just because of Darcy's letter, or Nails's note, or because his girlfriend had officially dumped him in the most heinous way imaginable. I knew, because he'd overlooked a very significant detail concerning Nails. Normally Fun *obsesses* over details. Think of his graffiti. Think of the caricature of Headmaster Stanton he painted in the basement of the assembly hall—how he nailed the flab on those saggy cheeks with the exact folds and *everything*. Yet, in this case he missed the obvious.

Nails included the word *murdered* in his note.

How would Nails know Darcy had been murdered unless it was a lucky guess or he had some inside information? The Wellington cops—not privy to the e-mail or the letter—were beginning to assume that Darcy Novak had run away. The day after our discovery, I overheard Officer Jacobs saying to Stanton that she "could have joined the Peace Corps or won the lottery or reinvented herself as a whole different person." I couldn't blame him. Think of the possibilities. But Nails didn't. He only thought of one.

And Fun didn't notice.

Also, on a random note, I was pretty struck by Nails's grammar in that e-mail. Perfect syntax and punctuation. Kind of weird, especially since Nails is dyslexic, or a spoonerist, or whatever you call it. You should see the way I e-mail: no caps, all shorthand, lots of *dot dot dots* (they're called ellipses, right? That's what Nails and Fun call them). But as Fun said, even the worst boarding-school kids are articulate.

That's what I tried to focus on during those first few days of classes. Being articulate. Being Sheila Smith, haughty and aloof. Concentrating on picking up all those boarding-school quirks and obscure references ("prodigal" anyone?). It would have been negligent of me not to behave like one of those kids whom Darcy Novak wanted to save: the crazy ones who are stuck at Winchester and who make fun of it just so they don't lose their minds. I tried to focus on *being* fake so I wouldn't *feel* fake.

I tried to forget that Darcy Novak was real. But I couldn't.

I definitely couldn't forget the reality of Nails.

Was he just trying to screw with his mom in that e-mail? Or was it as Darcy wrote: Did he believe Stanton would read it? God knows I tried to screw with my parents every now and then, and we had a pretty *honest* relationship.

To complicate matters, we shared a class, Nails and I. Well, the three of us did: Miranda was in it too—third period. How to Write an Effective Haiku. The way it worked (if you could call it that) was pretty much the way I remembered free time from kindergarten: some initial ground rules, and then you were free to play. Miss George was our putative teacher. (Nails taught me that word. It means "so-called.") On the first day, she explained to us the basic foundation of haiku writing. Five syllables in the first line, seven syllables in the second line, then five again in the third.

One would assume that she'd read us some examples of "effective" haikus, or give us a little history as to their origin. She did neither. She said she'd save "context" for later, but for now she wanted our minds uncluttered.

For the next few days she sat at the head of the class, feet on her desk, buried in a book written in Japanese. We were free to do as we pleased, provided we ended the class with at least one Haiku.

Here's an example from Nails:

Good-bye Kirk Bishop
I would like you to leave school
Get out, get out; Go!

Miranda wrote as a response:

Why should Kirk leave us?
Maybe he knows what happened
Best he stays right here

To which Nails replied:

Haikus are quite dumb
But not as dumb as Miss George
Wouldn't you say so?

In the end, the best I could do was:

Darcy where are you?
Please turn up soon. We miss you.
You should be in Grease

So much for being articulate.

PART THREE

1 Fun receives a disturbing phone call from his father, and later, *Grease* auditions are announced at breakfast in the presence of police officers.

2 Nails inadvertently reveals that he knows the true identity of Sheila Smith. Three days later, Carli is called to perform onstage.

3 Time passes; Fun reflects; Carli regrets taking the stage; Nails blogs—and eventually, certain issues come to a boil in the basement of the school library.

4 The Book Society meets, whereupon Fun makes an extremely upsetting discovery.

5 Fun and Carli begin and conclude their investigation—in earnest.

6 The punch line

1

Fun receives a disturbing phone call from his father, and later, Grease auditions are announced at breakfast in the presence of police officers.

FUN

Carli and I came up with a plan the following week. Or rather, it came up with us.

Since I'd resigned myself to the possibility that my roommate and best friend might be a stranger (and by extension a murderer), I'd become an insomniac. It didn't help that Nails snored. A guilty person always sleeps best, right? That's what I remembered from Crime in Film, a moronic course I'd taken sophomore year, where *I* would often fall asleep and leave puddles of drool in my notebook.

Every morning I shivered in the darkness, listening to the

haunting rhythm of Nails's stuffed nose and thinking of the movie *The Usual Suspects,* where I'd heard that line. I'd attended maybe 20 percent of that class, tops. But I'd managed to go to that one, and also the one where *Fight Club* was screened: "When you have insomnia, you're never really awake, and you're never really asleep." That was my life.

On the fourth morning, at around 6 A.M., my cell phone rang. *BEE-BEE-BEEP!*

I jerked upright and, tossing the covers aside, dashed to my desk.

"Hello?" I answered in a terrible whisper.

"Hiya, Fun. It's your old man."

"Dad?" I clutched the cold phone against my hot face. Faint traces of sunlight were just beginning to illuminate the indigo sky. "It's three in the morning, LA time."

He chuckled. "I know. I'm just doing some last-minute location scouting for *Private Nights*. Long day. We're building a faux New England in LA."

"Why are you calling me?"

"Well, Sheila Smith and I spoke on the phone a few nights ago. Our conversation was a little peculiar. I wanted to talk to you about it."

I scratched the back of my boxer shorts in a semi-hallucinatory state. "Don't call her Sheila, Dad. It's embarrassing."

"Don't sound so oppressed," he chided with a cluck of his tongue. "Look, Carli mentioned that Nails's ex-girlfriend is missing. I've done a little research. And I think I've come up with an angle for this whole situation."

"Fine." At this point, I only wanted to humor him. The best thing to do was to let him talk. It would end the conversation much faster.

"You're a good-looking kid, Fun."

Suddenly I was very aware that I was in my boxers in a darkened dorm room on the phone with my father. "I'm a . . . what?"

"You know that I've always wanted gritty realism for this program—"

"Dad, if you send a camera crew here, I'm running away. I mean it. I appreciate everything you've done to make sure I could graduate, but that's too much."

"Who said anything about sending a camera crew?"

I plopped down on my behind, leaning against the door. "I know how you think, Dad," I moaned. "You just said yourself that you'd come up with an 'angle' for your show. A girl is *missing.* It's serious. Darcy has nothing to do with entertainment or some kind of new reality TV project you're pitching."

He snorted. "Such the young philosopher."

"I'm serious!" I barked. Luckily, Nails kept snoring.

"Calm down," Dad soothed. "All I'm saying is that if Carli Gemz is dead set on finding out what happened to this girl, it doesn't have to be a disaster. So long as you make sure Carli doesn't reveal her true identity. If she stays Sheila Smith, I think you've got something here. Something that can actually be positive, that can make a difference."

I gazed at Nails's belly, slowly rising and falling under his blanket in the dim blue half-light. "I really wish I knew what the hell you were talking about," I mumbled.

"Don't be dense, Fun." He slipped in to that old familiar tone, the tone he used when I first started getting caught for spray-painting my name on overpasses. "You work with *Sheila* to find out what happened to Darcy. Not Carli. And you know what? If you do that, I'll tear up the agreement you signed for me about your relationship with her."

I laughed. I couldn't help myself. "You mean I'm free to hook up with her? Gee, Dad. What *have* you been smoking? Or is this a Drink and Dial?"

"Clever! This is exactly what I'm talking about. You ever see the show *Remington Steele*? It was an 80s show. I worked on it for a bit as a locations scout when I was just getting started. It's analogous to what I'm thinking, but gender reversed. The two leads had a chatty rapport, and each picked up on clues that the other one missed. Also, it's a perfect example of how romance blossoms from mutual hostility. Everyone wonders, Will these two ever hook up? Remains to be seen, but the action is rife with comic tension and moments of tender bonding. And . . . oh, my God! If we decided to use Carli's real name, we could call the show *Fun and Games*! Get it?"

"Listen to yourself right now, Dad," I croaked. "Seriously. You're a caricature of yourself. Who *talks* like you?"

"Remington Steele," he said.

"Remington Steele talks the way you do?"

"No, *Remington Steele* is the name of the *show*, you putz," he snapped. "I just told you that. It starred Pierce Brosnan. One of the Bonds. It's the show where *he* got his start. Just like you can get yours. Brosnan plays a phony sleuth. He was an actor playing an actor playing a detective. Well actually he was an actor playing a jewel thief playing a detective . . . but the point is, you're Stephanie Zimbalist."

He'd lost me at *putz*. "Bye, Dad," I said.

Snapping my cell phone shut, I glanced out the window. The sky had brightened during that brief surreal exchange. Another sleepless night down the drain . . .

Nails rolled over on his side. "What time is it, dude?" he groaned.

"Too early," I said.

"Yeah, I know. Who was that?"

"It was my dad." I stood slowly and stretched, my knees creaking, then tossed my phone on my bed.

"At least it wasn't a telemarketer."

I laughed. The sound died in my throat. Nails yawned.

"You know, I think I'm going to start my own Darcy Novak blog. I'll post it on the Winchester Web site. I've seen a few, and they all suck. Everybody has a theory, but none are legit. I'll run the whole thing as her grieving ex-boyfriend, and Kirk and I can debate each other, like on those right-wing talk shows. Something like that would probably look good on a college application, right?"

I turned to him. "Nails?"

"Yeah?"

"Swear to me that you didn't have anything to do with this."

"With what?"

"With Darcy!"

He rolled over. "Good night."

"If you absolutely swear—"

"Are we in the third grade?" he snapped. "Hope to die, stick a needle in my eye? I can't believe you'd stoop so low, Fun. How much have we been through together? Huh? Remember that time sophomore year, when Miles O'Shay wanted to pummel you and I preached it out of him with my nonviolent schtick? And after all *that*, you think I could surt humbody—I mean, hurt somebody—especially Darcy?"

I bowed my head. It was a stupid conversation. So I opened our closet door and began fumbling in the darkness for the paint cans I'd hidden in the back. A familiar, uncontrollable urge was consuming my brain and limbs.

"What are you doing?" Nails demanded.

"I need to get out of here. I need to clear my head and get some fresh air. I need to go tag something."

He was quiet for a moment. "Okay. But be careful." He curled up in a fetal position, pulling the covers over his head. "There may be a killer on the loose."

Carli

The dining hall was always at its most depressing early in the morning. It could have been my mood. It was cold for September, wasn't it? Miranda had lent me a fuzzy, homemade sweater. *Her* mood was great. Her crying days seemed to be over. The sweater hung off me like a potato sack, down past the hem of my skirt. But I appreciated the gesture. To be honest, waking up with girlish banter about borrowing clothes was preferable to another drippy conversation about Miranda's infatuation with Nails.

Too bad I'd thrown out Darcy's letter in the depths of a shame spiral. Miranda might think differently if she saw it.

What made this morning particularly dismal, however, was that Headmaster Stanton was waiting for us all. He stood at the lectern in front of the buffet, grim and reeking of sleeplessness, in a black suit. The lingering fog obscured the sunlight streaming through the huge bay windows. In short: a harbinger of doom.

More than a week had passed, and there was still no sign of Darcy. I'd given up sneaking off to the taped-off area by the laundry building, searching for clues that the police might have missed. All I found were Marlboro butts. And no way was I ever returning to her room.

As Miranda and I trudged toward the steaming buffet trays, I waved at Headmaster Stanton and mouthed, "Hi." He waved back, unsmiling. My Prada boots squished on something. I glanced down. It was a piece of hamburger bun. No surprise: the floor hadn't been mopped all week. Franny's Free-4-all had a much more thorough custodial staff than Winchester. I knew, because I *was* that staff.

I don't think I ever missed Grizz as much as I did at that moment.

Kirk, Sarah, and Mary stood a few feet ahead in line. Stale cigarette smoke clung to their clothes; I could smell it. I watched as all three scooped piles of eggs onto their plates. Mary giggled, plucking a cement-colored sausage from a bowl with a pair of tongs and wagging it in Kirk's face. He giggled and took a bite. Maybe I would take Jonathan Newport's advice and shed a few pounds. Yes. If I didn't, I would barf.

"Hey, are you all right?" Miranda asked. "You look a little wan."

Wan? "Uh . . . I'm fine. Just tired. I think I'll skip the hot breakfast."

"Cool. Save me a seat." She stood on her tiptoes. "Look! There's Nails and Fun." She pointed at a darkened corner in the rear of the cafeteria.

"I'll see you there," I said, hurrying over.

An interesting point of fact: Nails hadn't bothered to shower or change his clothes since the first day of school. Or maybe he just owned several "James Brown Sex Machine" T-shirts. It could be that he simply didn't trust Corleone Cleaners. Fun was wearing that Iron Maiden T-shirt again too. He sat slumped on the table, food untouched, head resting in the crook of his arm.

"Is it okay if Miranda and I sit here?" I asked.

"Does the Pope crap in the woods?" Nails answered cheerily, his eyes glued to Miranda's butt. He hopped up and grabbed his empty glass. "I'm gonna say hi to her."

Fun glanced up at me, bleary eyed. "He really isn't like this all the time."

"I guess I'll have to trust you on that." I sat across from him.

He forced himself to sit up straight. "You know, I've been

thinking about something Kirk said last week," he whispered, speaking low and fast. "It's been bothering me, because it didn't make a whole lot of sense."

"What's that?"

"He said that Stanton might have called Darcy right before she disappeared, pretending to be somebody else."

My eyes narrowed. "I don't get it. Who was he pretending to be?"

"A Hollywood agent. Somebody who wanted to sign her and yank her out of school and send her to be a famous actress." His eyes met mine. "To be like you. It's kind of a weird coincidence, don't you think? Seeing as he's the only one besides me who knows who you are."

I swallowed. "But why—" I broke off as Nails returned. "Hey, mind if I ask you something, Fun?" I asked in a phony voice. "Are you really an Iron Maiden fan?"

"Nah, I stole this T-shirt from Nails."

I almost smiled. "So you're a criminal."

"Yeah, but at least I admit it." Fun jerked his head toward the nearest window. "Speaking of which, have you seen my latest work? I did it this morning. Nails, I think you'll appreciate this too."

Painted in Gothic lettering on the back of the assembly hall, barely visible through the trees, was:

If cops are gonna hang out here
I wanna get mirandized

A strange, not-so-pleasant tingle squirmed in the pit of my stomach. It was probably just the smell of the institutional eggs. I ignored it before I could consider too deeply what Fun's graffiti meant. "Nice," I said.

"Skipping breakfast, Sheila?" Nails asked. He slumped into his chair and chugged some orange juice, smacking his lips. "Some say it's the most important meal of the day."

"Well, Fun's dad says I should lose some weight," I answered without thinking.

Nails laughed and twirled his fork. "Fun's dad said that? I mean, I know he and your dad are friends or whatever . . . but that's pretty harsh."

Uh-oh. I shot a quick glance at Fun. He was glaring at Nails, his eyes ice cold. In that instant, I knew. *Fun had told Nails who I really am.* Of course he did. If I were stuck in the same impossible situation as Fun, I would have confided in a best friend too. Otherwise I would have gone completely crazy. The problem was that this made our collective situation a whole lot trickier. Would Nails tell Miranda now?

"You know how rude my dad is, Nails," Fun stated in a flat voice. "He's an equal-opportunity jerk. But speaking of TV producers, Car—Sheila, I wanted to ask you about this show he mentioned."

"Carsheela?" Nails mocked. He dug back into his plate of eggs. "Finally, someone else with a speech impediment."

Fun pretended not to notice. "I wanted to ask you, Sheila: Have you ever heard of the TV show *Remington Steele*?"

The unpleasant tingle returned. I couldn't help but feel that a storm was brewing. "Uh . . . yeah, I have," I replied, struggling to focus. "It starred Pierce Brosnan and Stephanie Zimbalist. It was about a guy with a shady past who pretends to be a private investigator, because the *real* private investigator can't get any work because she's a woman. It ran from 1982 to 1987. In the pilot—"

Fun and Nails were both grinning at me. My cheeks felt hot. "What?"

Fun shook his head. "Nothing. I'm just impressed."

"Me too," Nails said. "Were you on that show or something?"

"Morning, guys!" Miranda cried. She scooted into the chair beside me, her tray loaded with every single breakfast item imaginable, down to a stale-looking croissant. "Hey, listen. I just bumped into Kirk Bishop in the food line. He wanted to remind us that the first meeting of the Book Society is a week from tomorrow night. He wanted to make sure we're all reading *The Human Stain.* He's really excited that we're all joining."

Nails snickered. "I'm sure he is. He wants—"

A screech of feedback blared from the buffet area. The four of us winced.

"Sorry," Headmaster Stanton announced, his voice booming. He tapped the microphone. "Good morning. I'll make this brief."

Several chubby, freshly shaven police officers joined him at the lectern, all with the same blank expressions.

"Lieutenant George Jacobs and his associates from the Wellington Police Department are here. We would like to talk with the following students. If you hear your name called, please report to me immediately. Your teachers will be notified in case you miss any classes." Headmaster Stanton hesitated and glanced at one of the officers, who nodded. "Kirk Bishop, Hilton James, and Sarah Ryder. Thanks."

I stopped breathing. There was a split second of funeral-parlor silence, as if nobody knew how to react. Then, all at once, hushed murmurings broke out everywhere.

The volume rose fast, echoing off the cafeteria walls. Miranda, Fun, and I turned to Nails, our jaws slack. He didn't seem to notice. He kept right on eating, shoving eggs into his mouth as if he'd been starved for weeks.

"People, *please* calm down," Headmaster Stanton commanded, raising his palms. "We're doing everything we can to find Darcy. We . . . uh . . . well, we all know Darcy is a lock for the role of Sandy in this semester's production of *Grease*, so once we find her, we know we'll get her onstage as soon as we can. Auditions start tomorrow! Please see Mr. Hines in his office in the arts and theater building if you're interested . . ."

His voice was lost in the crowd. He clicked off the microphone and shrugged at the police officers, all of whom shook their heads in embarrassment.

Nails hurled his fork onto his plate with a loud *clink*, a disgusted look on his face.

"Quite a performance! Stanton has truly outdone himself."

He shoved himself away from the table and dropped his napkin on the floor. "I guess I'll catch you guys later."

I watched him go.

"Maybe I'll try out for *Grease* too," Miranda said quietly. "Being in the play would be a great way to honor Darcy."

Fun shot me a blank glance.

Of all the strange and offensive . . . I'd been wrong about my roommate. She was not what she seemed at first glance either. No, she was hiding something too—that she wasn't endearing, she was a creep.

I leaned across the table. "Hey, Fun, would you mind showing me your graffiti up close?" I asked. "I mean, neither of us is eating, and it's probably best to look at it while the cops are *inside*, don't you think?"

I don't think I'd ever seen him look more relieved. "Wise plan," he said.

2

Nails confesses that he indeed knows the true identity of Sheila Smith, and three days later, Carli is called to perform onstage.

Fun

I took a moment to collect myself as I stood with Carli in the shade of the willow tree next to the assembly hall. With the Darcy hullabaloo, my latest tag would probably last longer than some of the others, maybe even the rest of the week. Good. The black gothic lettering stood out in bold contrast against the red brick. I was pretty proud of it.

"So, you wanna get Mirandized, huh, Fun?" Carli asked after a while.

"Not anymore." I glanced at my watch. The fog was starting to burn off. Physics for Poets started in fifteen minutes. "Not like

Nails might be, right now."

"Do you *like* Miranda?" she prodded.

I raised my shoulders. I didn't really. At first, I'd thought she was cute and different. And I'd been sort of turned on by how she'd hooked up with her gym teacher. But what she'd just pulled back there, with the *Grease* try-outs . . . that was weird. And I was pissed at how she seemed so flirtatious with Nails. I was even more pissed at how she evidently preferred him to me. But did that mean I liked her? Maybe it meant I despised her. Or that I was jealous. She definitely did occupy my thoughts, though.

"Sorry," Carli muttered. "You don't have to answer."

"I'm still thinking," I said.

She laughed softly. "You boarding-school kids do that a lot."

"Yeah, I know. We also *think* about thinking. You should make a note of it for your character. We're all super-meta."

"Can I ask you something else, Fun?"

"Sure. Shoot. As long as it's meta."

"Does Nails really have a speech impediment?"

"It only kicks in when he's agitated. It's sort of a . . ."

"A tell?" she suggested.

"What's that?"

"Nothing," she murmured. She rubbed the sides of her arms with her floppy sleeves. What was she *wearing* right now? Tall black boots, leggings, and an oversized wool sweater that looked like it had been stitched on a farm in the middle of nowhere by an inbred family, or the comic-movie version of one. To be generous, the gray argyle pattern did highlight the gray flecks in her eyes. I hadn't really noticed her eyes before.

"Oh, by the way, my dad called this morning," I said.

"Uh-oh. He's pissed at me, isn't he? I bet he's gonna fire me."

My lips curled in a grin. "You're pretty insecure, aren't you?"

"Who isn't?" she shot back.

"Good point." A gust of wind blew. The willow branches swayed above us. I jammed my hands in my pockets, wishing I'd worn a jacket. Goose bumps rose on my arms. "No, he's not going to fire you. He called because he's cool with us trying to figure out what happened to Darcy. He's even—" I bit my lip. I was about to say, *He's even cool with us hooking up*, only as a point of fact. But Carli might take that the wrong way. Instead I finished: "He's even worried about her, himself."

Carli shook her head and drew closer. "You're lying," she said.

"No I'm not! Ask Nails. My dad called at six this morning."

"You're lying about something," she stated. "Or you're holding something back. I can see these things, Fun. I'm an actress."

Blood rushed to my face, but I couldn't help smiling. "I think he wants to revise the whole premise of the show. He wants you to try to find out what happened to Darcy. I mean not *you,* you. *Sheila*, you. Or maybe *you*, you." I let out a deep breath. "As soon as he says 'reality' or 'meta,' I tune out."

Carli burst out laughing. Then she shook her head, scrunching her eyebrows. "Are you serious? He wants to make *Private Nights* a detective show now? *The Facts of Life* meets *Remington Steele*?"

"People really talk like that in Hollywood, don't they? I

mean, like, people our age. People who aren't even old enough to vote."

"Don't get me started." Carli groaned. She absently tugged at one of her pigtails. "I can picture what was running through your dad's mind." She broke into a used-car-salesman voice. "Care for wacky adventure? Then watch *Private Nights*! Starring Carsheela Smith, a neurotic seventeen-year-old actress, and Fun, her delinquent and indentured seventeen-year-old assistant! Forced together through circumstances beyond their control, they find themselves embroiled in a wild mystery they couldn't have possibly imagined! Think *Prep* meets *Hoot*, but with *Harry Met Sally heart!*"

I gaped at her and then started applauding. She deserved it. She'd pulled a Darcy. If my dad fired this girl from his lame show, he was an idiot.

Carli took a bow. "Thank you, thank you."

"Well, not so fast. If I'm going to be your co-star, I think we need superpowers."

"Superpowers?"

"Yeah. I mean, if this program is really gonna take off, we need to appeal to the comic-geek fan base, right? It's *huge.* It'll bring our market share up by double-digit percentage points in the first quarter, at least."

Carli seized my chin and kneaded it for a moment. "And they said you were just a pretty face," she cooed, baby-talk style. "Love it! So here's what I'm thinking for you: You're this, like, incredible artist, and you can paint anything—graffiti, caricature, murals, what have you. Instead of your average human's dull eye, you have this *magical ability* to spot all kinds of tiny details that normal people totally miss. Oh, and you're never afraid to wise off to authority figures at your own peril. Which is pretty impressive, because most of the time, you're a stupid screwup."

I laughed. "What about you? What are your superpowers?"

"Well, all sorts. I'm an expert soup chef—not to be confused with *sous* chef, because I'm the boss of the kitchen. I have an encyclopedic knowledge of TV and movie history. I'm better than the Internet. I can usually tell when someone is lying, too. Plus, I can cry on demand!"

"Brilliant! Listen, we are gonna take the entertainment—" I broke off, catching a glimpse of Nails ambling down the path toward us. The lunatic moment of euphoric amnesia vanished. Back to reality. I jammed my hands back into my pockets. Carli hugged herself again, the light fading from her eyes. Her sleeves flopped in the wind.

"Hey, Nails," I called. "How'd it go?"

Nails peered over his shoulder, his lips set in a sour arc. He picked up his pace. "I'm not sure," he said with a sigh, leaning against the trunk of the willow tree.

"What do you mean?" Carli asked.

"Stanton and that cop, Jacobs, wanted to talk to me separately."

"Which cop is Jacobs?" Carli asked.

"The one on the radio last week, the fat one," Nails said.

"They're all fat," she said.

"The *obese* one, compared to our sticklike bodies, okay, Hollywood?"

Hollywood? I cringed.

"They pulled me into the kitchen," he went on, "and asked me point-blank if I'd been hawking sir before school started—I mean, stalking her. So I pointed out that I wasn't the only one at school early—Kirk and Sarah and Mary were here too—and it was just a coincidence that I bumped into her. But Stanton wouldn't buy it . . ."

I tuned out. It was horrible. I should have been hanging on his every word, trying to console him. For some reason, once again, all I could think was, *The way he pronounces Stanton is more like "Stan'n." And with a flat "a": "eh." "Stehn'n."* Carli had planted a terrible seed of suspicion in my brain. *If he's trying to hide an accent, what else has he been trying to hide all these years?* Part of me wanted to extract that seed and flush it down the toilet immediately. But another part of me wanted to tend to it, to see what poisoned fruit it would bear.

"What else happened?" Carli asked.

"So the cops brought Sarah and Kirk into the kitchen. Then Miranda came in too. And they all started talking about *Grease*—Stanton, the cops. It was like, 'Oh, we're not gonna find the dead girl today, might as well move on.' Did you know that Sarah and Mary are trying out for the play this year? They're both trying out for Sandy. And so is Miranda. It was sick. It went from an interrogation to, like, a pre-audition."

I shifted on my feet.

"I think the three of us should go to the auditions," Nails finished, his voice tight. "I'm telling you, I think Stanton knows what happened to Darcy. The way he's acting . . . I think he's worried that now that she's gone, Hines's precious play is going to be ruined, another black mark against Winchester. He's never paid this much attention to the play before."

"Are you sure?" Carli murmured. "Sounds like a stretch."

Nails threw his pale, bony arms in the air. "You don't know Stanton, Carli!"

Her eyes darted to mine. "Carli? Who's Carli? My name's Sheila."

Oh, crap. The color drained from my face. We stood in silence. My watch ticked. Carli kept right on smiling. Nails's skin turned a shade of white I wouldn't have believed possible. It was beyond chalk. He backed away, shaking his head at me. My heart speeded up.

"This Leesha Carli siznet brisket . . . Sheila Carli secret business . . . I'm sorry—"

"It's okay." Carli caught his arm. Then she grabbed mine. "No need to apologize. As long as neither of you two jackasses tells anyone else who I am. Got it?"

Nails and I both nodded. Her manicured nails nearly punctured my bicep.

"Good," she said. "Now, on to more pressing matters. If Nails is right about Stanton, I agree. We should go to the *Grease* auditions."

I frowned. "We should?" Nails's wild theory seemed like a

stretch to me too; harping on Stanton was a pretty convenient way to deflect attention from *himself.* "Why?"

"Because if Nails is right, Stanton will be at his *most* stressed at the audition. He'll be weak and vulnerable. That's when we should turn the tables."

Carli

For the next three days, Miranda wouldn't stop talking about how excited she was at the dim prospect of playing Sandy. She must have known she had a terrible voice, but she didn't seem to care. She was determined to beat the odds. It became the sole topic of discussion. As far as I could tell, she sincerely viewed the opportunity as some kind of tribute to Darcy. I could relate to the tribute part. I wanted to pay tribute as well.

Finding Darcy was maybe more of a fitting tribute, but who was I to judge?

Helping her rehearse was actually a fun little project. For the first time since I'd arrived at Winchester, I *was* being active; I *was* doing something nice for someone else, even if it was a lost cause. When we stuck to *Grease,* and didn't even mention Darcy, she annoyed me less. The shame spirals mellowed. They ceased to be overwhelming vortexes. Best of all, rehearsals kept her and Nails apart.

Sitting for hours on end in our tiny room, listening to her belt out off-key versions of "Summer Lovin'" and "Hopelessly Devoted" along with the CD, I became her de facto acting coach. (She did balk at my attempt to give her a makeover, unfortunately.)

The more she sang, the worse she sounded. Still, I focused on the positives. "You have a great presence!" "You nailed that vibrato in the last stanza!" "You're smiling more. Good!"

The night of the big tryout, she was shaking so much I thought she might get sick. She also decided to wear overalls and heels, much to my chagrin.

"You're gonna do fine," I said soothingly as we left.

She gulped, teetering on the paved path. "I'm nervous," she moaned.

"Don't be." I looped my arm around hers and tugged her forward. "Think of the competition. You'll blow Sarah and Mary out of the water. Think they have a vibrato?"

The Nicholas Barrington Center for the Theater and Arts stood in its own private nook, tucked away from the center of campus at the edge of the Winchester vineyards. I wasn't sure who "Nicholas Barrington" was, but his theater was definitely an anomaly compared to the rest of the school buildings. It was much newer, built of shiny white concrete with tinted floor-to-ceiling windows. It was *clean*, too. Even the wall-to-wall carpeting had been freshly vacuumed.

We arrived at the auditorium at 6:47 P.M., two minutes after auditions were due to start. It was already dark, except for the bright stage lights. Headmaster Stanton sat in the front row. Mr. Hines, the head of the drama department, sat at an upright piano, stage right, his bald head glistening under a spotlight. And in a tidy line behind him stood Sarah, Mary, and about eighteen girls I'd never seen before. Otherwise, it was deserted.

"Break a leg," I whispered.

"Thanks." Miranda squeezed my hand and hurried to the stage.

"Psst!"

Jesus. I jumped in surprise and then spun around, nearly falling over. Fun and Nails were right behind me, creeping into the back row. I quickly sat between them. I tried not to squirm. Poor Miranda! This was a catastrophe waiting to happen. If she didn't get the role of Sandy, she might have a shot at Frenchie, the bubble-headed beauty-school dropout.

"Why is it that Stanton and Hines are the only ones who ever get to decide who's in and who's out of the school play?" Nails whispered.

"You're asking me?" I whispered back.

"Shh!" Fun hissed.

Headmaster Stanton turned in his seat, glowering.

The three of us offered a feeble wave back.

Mr. Hines peered out from the stage. "Okay! Let's have our first Sandy, please!" He cleared his throat and wriggled his fingers over the keyboard. "Miranda Jenkins?"

She stepped out into the spotlight. I tried not to cringe. Overalls and heels! I'd begged her to wear one of my Diane von Furstenberg miniskirts; she'd declined. Still, she'd tucked some of her hair back in a barrette, which was cute. Not Sandy cute, but definitely Frenchie cute.

The room fell silent. Mr. Hines began to play. It was the soft, lilting melody of "Hopelessly Devoted." Not surprisingly,

Fun and Nails started cracking up. I scowled at them. They both chewed on their fists for the next excruciating thirty seconds. I held my breath. Blood rushed to my ears. *Please stop, please stop*—and then it was over.

"Woo-woo!!!" Nails cried.

The three of us jumped up and gave a standing ovation, purely from relief. Funny: It was probably the happiest I'd been at Winchester so far.

Mr. Hines didn't share our joy, though. Nor did Headmaster Stanton. Worse, Mr. Hines stared in my direction, directly at *me*. I glanced over my shoulder. Nobody was sitting behind us. Of course not: we were in the last row, against a cement wall.

I twisted back around and squinted at the stage.

"You, there," Mr. Hines called, shielding his eyes from the glare with his hand.

"Who, me?" I asked.

"Yes, you. Do you sing?"

Fun and Nails stopped smiling.

"I . . . well, a little," I said. My face flushed. "Not much."

"Why are you here, then?"

"Just to, um, check out the auditions, really," I lied. "I was curious. My roommate is trying out. I'm here for moral support."

"I see." He whispered something to Miranda, and then beckoned to me. "Come down here, please. It's Miss Smith, isn't it? Sheila Smith?"

"Yes, it is, but I don't know why I need to go down there—"

"Go!" Fun whispered furiously.

"Yeah, we don't want trouble!" Nails said, shoving me in the ribs. "We don't want Stanton to suspect anything."

I clambered out of our row and hurried down the aisle, fighting to ignore Headmaster Stanton's bewildered stare as I hoisted myself up onto the stage. *This is bad.* I'd forgotten how *hot* a theater stage is. On a TV soundstage, everything is always perfectly climate controlled. Here, there were just lights. My legs were shivering, but my forehead was already beginning to perspire.

"Your roommate insists you have a lovely singing voice," Mr. Hines stated. "Is that so? Because you're certainly attractive enough to play the role of Sandy."

Normally, hearing a comment like that from a bald old man would make me feel icky. But he'd brought his kids. Two little towheaded children dressed in ill-fitting cutoff shorts were scurrying around the prop room backstage—invisible to the audience—hurling plastic forks at one another. *Poor guy.* I let it slide.

"You would like to audition?" Mr. Hines asked. He phrased it more as a statement than a question. "*You* would like to audition."

I glanced at the rest of the girls trying out for the part.

Most of them looked like sophomores, or even freshmen. Lots of braces and bangs and plump cheeks, coupled with awkward, tall, skinny bodies. It wouldn't be fair.

Miranda scuttled toward me. She threw an arm around my shoulders and pulled me in for a hug. I was a little freaked; in spite of our recent closeness, we'd never been this intimate before. But this was the theater, in some ways the perfect place for intimacy.

"Just sing a song," she whispered. "Sing 'You're the One That

I Want.' They'll cast you for sure. Do it! Do it for Darcy Novak! If you're in, you'll be that much closer to her, maybe to finding out what happened to her. It can't hurt."

Maybe she was right. If I landed the role of Sandy, it would at least put in me in regular close contact with Headmaster Stanton—which meant I might have a better shot at ruling him in or out as a suspect. We were bound by my secret identity, too, and a bond was always good for breaking barriers. And if what Fun told me about his father's new idea for *Private Nights* was true, being in the school play would add a nice little twist. Either that or piss him off. It was a win-win.

"Um, okay." I smiled into the spotlights as Miranda dashed back to the wings. "Mr. Hines? Can you sing Danny Zuko's part in 'You're the One That I Want'? We can improvise the chorus harmonies toward the end."

He smiled confidently, sitting back down at the piano. "I think I can do that, Miss Smith. Let's take it from the top, shall we? Up-tempo. One-two-three-FOUR!"

3

Time passes; Fun reflects; Carli feels regret; Nails blogs—and circumstances come to a dangerous head in the basement of the school library.

Fun

Carli landed the role, of course. The contest was over as soon as she took the stage. Nails and I were floored. We kept mouthing, "OH, MY GOD," at each other. Dad had never mentioned that Carli could sing. *She'd* never mentioned it. It was weird. I mean; I know I'm a decent graffiti artist, but Carli has an exceptional gift. If I were that talented, I'd brag about it all the time. Afterward she kept shrugging it off and mumbling about how she wished she'd stayed in her room. Maybe she felt guilty about stealing the spotlight from Miranda.

Miranda didn't lose out completely, though. She was cast as

Marty, one of the Pink Ladies—the one who can't sing or dance. Sarah was cast as Frenchie. (Ha!) Mary was cast as Rizzo, which for some reason infuriated her.

"This play is so lame anyway," she muttered at the end of the night, stomping off to the woods to smoke an illicit cigarette. "It's like *West Side Story* meets *Hair,* but not in a good way. I'm just doing it to get material for my novel."

Kirk Bishop, of course, got exactly what he wanted.

When he sang "Sandy," I nearly barfed. I couldn't tell if he was overacting because he was pining for Darcy, or because he knew he *should* be pining for Darcy. He clamped his hands over his heart, staring up at the spotlights, his eyes rheumy. Talk about meta-meta. It was sick. But he could hold a tune, and even with the pimples and sunken cheeks, he looked good onstage. Of course, as Winchester's favorite son, he'd always been a shoo-in for the role of Danny Zuko anyway—the bad boy anti-hero. Now all the more tragic with a missing girlfriend . . .

We never did get a chance to pounce on Stanton. As soon as the audition ended, he and Mr. Hines disappeared out the backstage exit.

After that, the campus calmed down a little.

Two days, three days, four days . . . and still no Darcy.

The laundry area remained cordoned off, but the cops started showing up less and less. Darcy's name didn't come up as often either. At the dining hall and on the paths, I overheard more of the same old conversation: "We're gonna turn the well out by the distillery into a massive gravity bong" . . . "Hey, is it cool if I copy your calculus homework?" . . . "I gotta adjust my Ritalin dosage" . . . It felt just like last year. It was wrong. Worse, I couldn't seem to get Carli alone. Rehearsals started taking up all her time. We managed to sneak in a few hushed phone conversations, but they never came to anything; mostly she wanted to know if my dad had called to check up on her.

The only real difference on campus: The new laundry service provided ample opportunity for pranks. Fake poop, fake barf, fake everything, on the not-so-creative side. But even Kirk seemed to forget why we had to send out our laundry to Corleone Cleaners in the first place.

"I packed my boxers with diarrhea made from dining-hall pudding!" he boasted.

Carli

There *was* one ingenious laundromat prank, courtesy of a group of freshman day students. According to Kirk Bishop, freshman day students rank the lowest on the Winchester social totem pole. By definition, they lived at home (i.e., they were locals and therefore assumed to be hicks. The haughty senior boarders like Kirk saddled them with the moniker "3-D.") But this year's bunch earned our eternal respect.

What happened was this:

A particularly reckless girl, Karen Wilson, stole her parents' SUV. She wasn't even licensed to drive. With the help of a few select friends, Karen loaded it with a massive Salvation Army haul. Together, they intercepted the very first Corleone Cleaners delivery and switched about thirty bags' worth of laundry. That glorious Monday morning, we were forced to roam the campus in frilly wedding gowns, boxers, top hats, and tattered overcoats.

For a few surreal hours, the whole campus turned into a Magritte painting gone horribly awry. All the world was indeed a stage, and all of us were players . . . even more so than usual.

I also remember that on that day, I didn't hear Darcy Novak's name mentioned once. Winchester managed to completely forget her for a while. Not that this was a positive.

Another downside to the prank was that a lot of kids stopped sending their clothes to Corleone Cleaners. Some even stopped changing their clothes. The worst offender by far was Nails. He refused to take off that same flimsy James Brown Sex Machine shirt—"as an ironic protest," he said. Though he never clarified what was ironic, or what he was protesting—the fact that people were forgetting about Darcy?

Maybe they were. Nobody talked about her, except Miranda. Whenever there was a take-five during *Grease* rehearsals, whenever I brought up Darcy's name, Kirk and Sarah and Mary would vanish for a cigarette break. That generally left me alone with Miranda and C. J. Anderson, the little curly-haired twerp who'd been cast as Kenickie. He didn't feel much like talking about Darcy either. He seemed much more interested in staring at Miranda's cleavage.

But if people weren't talking, they were definitely *thinking*.

Fun was right. People thought about thinking here. It was the world capital of internal conversation. Everybody mumbled to themselves on the paths. I noticed *myself* mumbling once, about the mumbling. But whether that was due to Darcy's disappearance, or because Winchester kids tended to fantasize or to replay arguments they'd wished had gone better, or if they were just plain *weird*—I couldn't say.

FUN

Here's an illuminating IM exchange I had with Carli one night while Nails was playing Frisbee with Miranda in the quad before dinner:

> ME: hey has miranda said anything about darcy recently?
>
> CARLI: no. im freaked out. darcy's been missing over 2 weeks now.
>
> ME: me too and nails doesn't want to talk about it. i barely even see the kid anymore. can't stop thinking about the call kirk bishop thought came from stanton. it has to mean something
>
> CARLI: idk. u think he made it up???
>
> ME: good point
>
> CARLI: why would stanton pretend to be an agent? what could he want from darcy?
>
> ME: idk—coincidence is 2 weird. sumbody is pulling the strings behind the scenes idk who. it has to do with money.
>
> CARLI: you sound like a character from the godfather ☺

ME: ha, ha

CARLI: meant as a compliment. or is it complement???

ME: compliment with an "i." see! ur vocabulary is improving as ur morals slowly disappear. well done sheila

CARLI: thx.

ME: think this dialogue will make it into the new improved tv show?

CARLI: who knows? how meta of you to ask

ME: ur learning sheila smith. good for you.

Carli

As the first Book Society meeting drew near, Miranda lost interest in rehearsing for the role of Marty. I could understand. She couldn't act, let alone sing or dance. Like me, she also wanted to see what fireworks would ignite when Nails and Kirk were stuck once again in the same room together. They'd long since stopped sharing the same cafeteria table, or even showing up at the same times for meals. From what I could tell, Nails stopped eating, period.

Miranda's motivations for wanting to get Nails and Kirk together were the polar opposite of mine, obviously. She was increasingly convinced that Kirk was the guilty party, or at least that he knew something we didn't. *He* was the most recent boyfriend. *He* was the sociopath. If stuck with Nails, he would snap. I still had my bets on Nails. Then again, I hadn't made out with him. But I was just as anxious for the Book Society meeting as she was.

Mostly, I was depressed.

What was I thinking, taking the stage that night? I shouldn't be Sandy! Darcy should! I should have bolted when Mr. Hines called me up.

I spent a lot of time imagining Darcy and Kirk together on stage. They could have had a whole Katharine Hepburn / Spencer Tracy vibe going. Well, maybe more of a Tom Cruise / Katie Holmes vibe: the weirdo and the hot chick.

Kirk could sing, though. I was actually a little surprised. To hear Fun tell it, Kirk was a degenerate, and nothing more. He didn't *look* healthy. Then again, Spencer Tracy didn't look terribly healthy either. And as Winchester had taught me: Who can tell what a person is really like on the inside? Nails looked like death too.

Hey, I'm sure even Hitler had some redeeming qualities. Hitler could paint pretty well. They even made a movie about Hitler's life as a young artist: *Max,* with John Cusack. I saw it. It wasn't that bad. Fun would probably enjoy it. It was pretty dark (duh), but the performances were amazing, and I bet Fun would relate to being an outcast with the one saleable skill of painting. Not to equate Fun with Hitler.

Jesus. I can't even believe I went there. Whatever. Fun knows what I mean.

The only negative about the Book Society: C. J. Anderson asked if he could join, too. I wasn't exactly in a position to refuse him. Kirk was president. His response?

"Welcome, dude!"

Fun

Nails did end up starting a blog in Darcy's honor. Stanton wouldn't allow him to post it on the school's site (no big surprise), so Nails decided to set up on his own. He named it honor of his favorite catchphrase. It provided him a forum to rant about how nobody cared about Darcy, and also to assert that he was simultaneously the martyr and prime suspect. Like everything he wrote, it was either ingenious or idiotic, or both.

NOT THAT I'M GOING ANYWHERE WITH THIS . . .

Welcome!

9.22

Welcome to the official blog of Hilton James, a suspected murderer at the Winchester School of the Arts. The purpose of this blog is to find Darcy Novak. So, how's it going? All right, let's dispense with the pleasantries. Help me! Remember when our treasonous forty-third president, George W. Bush, said, "Bring 'em on" to the Islamo-fascists? People, I never thought I'd adopt the cowboy bravado of Dubya, but for those of you who know where Darcy Novak is, I offer the same challenge!

****

Comments: 2

1) u r a pathetic and a loser and i think you did it

—modestmousefan33

2) YOU ARE PATHETIC AND A LOSER AND I THINK YOU DID IT TOO.
—GREENDAYFAN48

No, you're the pathetic losers
9.24
Hi there again. Seems like some of you softies out there don't care about the Ruth. Maybe you can't handle the Ruth. No, that's not a misspelling. And don't blame my mental defect, because I honestly believe that one or both of you two bee-yatches may be Ruth James of Greenwich Connecticut. Am I right? Am I wrong? By the way: happy September 11. I know it was thirteen days ago, but as a society we've gotten to the point where we can say that. Or is that offensive? I wish you both a Happy Pearl Harbor Day, in advance!!! ☺ Is that morally acceptable? Is that appropriate behavior? You tell me.
****
Comments: 2
1) wrong on all counts
—modestmousefan33
2) WRONG ON ALL COUNTS
—GREENDAYFAN48

All right, so come to the first *Grease* script read-through in room B-4 in the library

9.25

Seems like neither or both of you is my mother, seeing as I had the following private conversation with my mother (and I hope you appreciate my indiscretion):

"I want you to meet Zack," she says. "He just got out of juvie."

"Who is Zack?" I ask.

"Our neighbor's son," she says.

"Mom, don't worry. I know enough guys."

"I'm introducing you to Zack because he can tell you what prison is like."

"If Zack was a chick, I'd be much more psyched to meet her."

"But I've told Zack's parents great things about you, even though you're a murderer."

"I'm sure you have. All those lies might finally start to pay off."

Kids, if I can share this with you, the least you can do is come to the first *Grease* script read-through! It's going to double as a Book Society meeting, thanks to Sheila Smith. Fun and I have been assigned to build and paint the trickier props again this year. btw: Here's a new feature. Feel free to contribute! ☺

Current Mood: Homicidal.

What I'm listening to: Evil Dead

Album: Scream Bloody Gore

Artist: Death

****

Comments: 2

1) i will be there cuz im in the chorus. u r not funny.

—modestmousefan33

2) I WILL BE THERE IM IN THE CHORUS TOO AND I DON'T THINK YOU ARE FUNNY. CURRENT MOOD: HOMICIDAL

—GREENDAYFAN48

Carli

It's true: I petitioned Headmaster Stanton (secretly) and Mr. Hines (openly, as my alter-ego, Sheila Smith) to combine the first two script readings with the first two meetings of the Book Society. The two groups were pretty much the same, anyway. Besides, I hadn't read *The Human Stain.* I didn't want to try to fake my way through another charade. I'd reached the point of nervous exhaustion. It was a good thing Jonathan Newport was on the West Coast. If he saw me . . . *Jesus.* My skin was sallow. I had bags under my eyes. I actually counted two zits on my neck (of all places).

He did call, however, at dawn the morning of the first Book Society meeting. Luckily, Miranda was washing up for breakfast.

"Jonathan?" I whispered, cupping the phone against my ear. "It's four in the morning there, for God's sake."

"Is it true?" he demanded. He didn't bother with hello.

"Is what true?"

"That you're playing Sandy in Winchester's production of *Grease*? I just got off the phone with Headmaster Stanton." There was some muffled fumbling, then a few muted curses. "You're playing the lead role in the *high-school musical*!"

"Uh . . ." Blood rushed to my face. So much for keeping a low profile and not attracting attention to myself. I'd violated my contract. I'd probably be fired. Relief coursed through me. Freedom! "Well, I said I would. But opening night is December twelfth, and I won't even be there then, so—"

"Okay," he interrupted. "No need to panic. This might solve some problems."

"I'm not panicking. What kind of problems?"

"Principal photography has been postponed until December," he said. "And—"

"It *has*?" I shouted. Now I *was* panicking. I stared at my tiny, stuffy, little room, a room that was the size of my walk-in closet back home, a room I shared with a disturbed girl who might very well be falling in love with a killer. "Does that mean I'll have to stay here until then?"

He laughed. "You just said you got the lead role in the musical."

"Well . . . yes. And I'm sorry. But I didn't say I'd *perform* in it. I figured Mr. Hines could give it to the understudy, or my roommate. Why has the schedule been postponed?"

"Script rewrite. But listen, Carli, I think this might be just the thing. You and Fun can try to solve this case of the disappearing girl or whatever—"

"Or whatever?" I barked. "Listen to you! She isn't disappearing. She's disappeared! Darcy Novak has been missing for three weeks! She's probably dead! And Kirk, or Headmaster Stanton, or Nails, or—"

"Shhhhhh, sweetie," he cut me off again, sounding uncannily like Ari Gold, Jeremy Piven's character from *Entourage.* I knew the impersonation was deliberate, too. Meta-Meta. "Relax. Use this. Use it to hone your acting chops. When it comes time for the big play, I'll make sure a lot of bigwigs are in the audience. It'll be like they just 'happened' to discover you. You know what I'm saying?"

I hung up before I even realized what I was doing. My thumb seemed to click on the END button of its own accord. But that was fine. *Fein.* I punched in her number.

A hoarse voice answered: "Hello?"

"Dr. Fun—I mean, Dr. Fein?"

"Carli? It's four in the morning."

"I know, but I really need to talk. I'm sorry."

She yawned. "Don't worry about it. Let me just find my glasses . . . There—and my notebook . . . good. So, what's going on? Did you sleep with your boss's son?"

My eyes narrowed. "*Excuse* me?"

"You just called me Dr. Fun."

"Yeah, but that was . . . that was . . ." I was too flustered to continue.

"A Freudian slip?" Dr. Fein joked dryly. "Don't worry about it. So, if you didn't sleep with your boss's son, what's the crisis?"

I shook my head, listening for the sound of the shower down

the hall. Miranda might suddenly reappear. "The crisis is . . . well, you know that this girl has disappeared. And her boyfriend and her ex-boyfriend are both involved in the play . . . I mean, her current boyfriend is starring in it and her ex is building the sets, and they're both in this club called the Book Society, so the thing is, I convinced the drama teacher, Mr. Hines, to combine the first meetings, just so I could observe them together in the same place—"

"Carli?"

"Yes?"

"Breathe. You're in a shame spiral."

I let out a deep breath. "You're right. Sorry."

"Don't apologize. You apologize far too often. When is this play?"

"In December."

"I see, and you'll have rehearsals up until then. And in the meantime you'll be rehearsing for *Private Nights,* as well . . ." She sighed. "Try to steer clear of this murder investigation, if you can. If you want to be an actress, then pursue it. This is certainly a difficult role. But remember what I said. This is not the healthiest situation, is it?"

I sat there, holding the phone. I considered hanging up and calling my mom and dad. But I couldn't. I was going to see this thing through. What better way to learn to act naughty than by embracing all the insanity as my own?

"You're right," I said. "It isn't healthy at all." And with that, I hung up.

Fun

Carli brought soup to the first Book Society and *Grease* cast-and-crew meeting that Monday night. Homemade soup; I kid you not. She'd spent the entire afternoon in her dorm room, preparing both vegetarian alphabet and split pea with ham in two tiny hotpots, so people "would have a choice." The jury is still out on whether this was saintly or psychotic. Maybe she really did believe she had soup-oriented superpowers, per our discussion. Maybe the strain had finally gotten to her and she'd cracked.

I must say, it *was* a true testament to Carli's skills that she convinced Mr. Hines to allow the first few Book Society meetings to "double up" with the first few *Grease* meetings, without arousing suspicion. Such a coupling only made sense in the context of Darcy. All the same players were involved: Me, Nails, Kirk, Sarah, Mary—and now Carli and Miranda. (C. J., too, I guess.) Plus, there were two random kids, a boy and a girl who looked like that couple I'd glimpsed on the football field.

They could have been the same couple, I supposed. They seemed scragglier, but everything becomes an Impressionist painting if you get far enough away from it. An image forms in your brain of what you think you've seen. The only way to prove yourself wrong is step in close, to shove your face into the chaos.

I also have to give Nails credit: Securing this room last year for Kirk was a coup. It was by far the nicest room in the library, furnished with plush couches and antique lamps, lined with maple bookshelves—tucked far below ground in the basement.

It could have used some fresh air, though. I'd handily forgotten Mr. Hines's chronic halitosis. The man sucked down garlic pills with near-religious fervor, claiming that they preempted any need for a flu shot. He was bald and never wore a hat, yet hadn't gotten sick in nearly a dozen winters. But maybe that was because nobody wanted to get close to him. Germs spread through proximity, through contact. Yes, sitting there in that tiny book-lined room, staring at all the friends and enemies and strangers, I finally figured out why his wife had left him. If I figured that out, maybe I could solve the Darcy mystery.

"Welcome, everyone," Mr. Hines said. "Thanks to Sheila, we've decided to try something new. In these opening, get-to-know-one-another, preliminary sessions—"

"Wait, hold on a second," Nails interrupted.

I shifted in my seat. The room was warm and fetid, and now that the door was closed, Mr. Hines's odor grew more powerful. I wasn't sure how long I could last.

"Yes, Hilton?" Mr. Hines asked.

Nails jabbed a finger toward the hippie football-field couple. "You two. What are your names?"

"Peter," the boy answered.

"Lisa," the girl said.

"Are you a Modest Mouse fan, by chance, Lisa?"

She shook her head. "I don't like emo. I like classic. Like Joplin."

"Scott or Janis?"

"Dude, you can do better than that," Lisa groaned.

Nails's grin widened. "Yeah, well, you know what Marx says."

"What are you talking about?"

"Marx! Pathetic! Even after all that, you missed the punch line? You're supposed to say, Groucho or Karl?" He slapped the table and punched me in the arm.

I winced. "Nails, you aren't making any sense."

"Yes I am. Just not to you. These guys are the bloggers. I'm sure of it. But that's fine. Sheila, I told you. You've brought us to Karmageddon."

Carli

For some odd reason, everyone refused my soup except for Fun, Nails, and Miranda. Why were the other kids such snoots? Even the underclassmen refused to partake—Peter and Lisa, the Janis Joplin couple. But they might have simply lost their appetite because Nails had flipped his lid, or because of the foul odor. Mr. Hines just seemed confused by the whole thing. Or at least by Nails.

Nails went straight for the split pea with ham.

He wolfed it down greedily, straight out of the container, spilling some, dribbling entire spoonfuls on his pants, all the while glaring at that boy and girl across the room.

"Hungry there, Nails?" Kirk snorted.

"Yes, I am. This is delicious, Sheila." He grinned at me. Little blobs of pea soup dripped from his chin. "Thanks."

My own grin faltered. "You're welcome."

"I'm serious. If I die, may I rest in peas," he joked.

"That's not funny," Kirk snapped. "Somebody may *be* dead."

Here we go . . .

"Funny you should mention that," Nails said. "Because I was just thinking the other day, you're a really great actor. In fact, you know who you remind me of, Kirk? You remind me of Robert Duvall's character in *Apocalypse Now.* Colonel Kilgore."

"What are you talking about?"

"You wander around in the middle of all this suffering with a huge smile on your face. Because somehow you know that none if it will touch you. It's like you have this instinctive knowledge that you're gonna be just fine. Even though you're the one who probably killed Darcy—"

"Nails, enough!" Mr. Hines snapped. He cleared his throat, then reached under the table and slapped down a huge pile of scripts: *Thwack!* "I don't want to hear another peep out of you. Otherwise, I'll ask you to leave. Understood?"

Kirk folded his arms across his chest. "I'd rather he leaves now."

"Fine." Nails upended the Tupperware container and swallowed the rest of my split pea with ham in one massive chug. Then he burped and stood, throwing the container to the floor with one hand while reaching into his back pocket with the other.

"But I do have a swan song." He yanked out a crumpled piece of notebook paper. "As this is a meeting of the Book Society, I'd just like to share some of my literary endeavors with you now. This is a poem I wrote, an original. It's more of a rap, really. It's called 'The Ballad of Winchester.'"

What do you want from me?
You run a kleptocracy

You rule by theft
My rhymes are deft
Has Darcy met her death?
Hines, you got bad breath
With those garlic pills
They don't cure your ills
Brush your teeth, son!
Or at least chew gum.
It's the polite thing to do
Like spraying Glade after you poo
Darcy sprayed . . . and so should you.

Nails glanced up.

"Hilton, please leave," Mr. Hines snapped.

"I know I sort of lost the rhythm and meter at the end there—"

"Now!" Mr. Hines shouted.

Nails sauntered out. His paper-thin James Brown Sex Machine T-shirt slipped down to expose a bony shoulder. He closed the door behind him. It took every single bit of self-control I had not to chase after him and give him a hug in that dark, subterranean hallway. I mean it: every single bit.

FUN

I returned that night to find Nails comfortably ensconced in bed, reading *The Human Stain*. I was beginning to feel lost. After Nails had left, we'd unanimously decided to postpone the first Book

Society meeting to clear our heads—at which point everyone bolted. We *all* felt lost. I spent forty-five minutes wandering the campus in a wordless fog, accompanied by Sheila and Miranda. I could only imagine what Kirk and Sarah and Mary were up to. Plotting how to get rid of Nails? Chain smoking? Both?

Before I could talk to Nails about his poem, or about his rash of unstable behavior in general over the past days, my cell phone rang. It was Carli.

"Who's that?" Nails asked nonchalantly. He grinned, his face buried in the novel's pages. "Sheila Smith of Saint Sancerre?"

Maybe Darcy was right to be scared of him.

I dashed into the bathroom. "Hello?"

"Fun-I've-been-robbed-I-mean-we've-been-robbed-oh-my-God—"

"Carli?" I gripped the phone tightly, so tightly that my knuckles turned white, "Slow down. You're hysterical."

"Sorry," she panted. "Listen, though. So Miranda and I get back from the meeting tonight. Our door is open. But the lights are out. So we flip on the lights, and we see . . . like, *half* our stuff is stolen. My date book, my makeup case, my cell phone, Miranda's hot pot . . . Fun, somebody is after us. Our room was ransacked. I lent Miranda half a pill of the emergency Xanax Dr. Fein prescribed, even though it was only meant for emergencies. I think she's asleep now. I . . . I . . ."

"Listen, Carli, it's okay. We'll tell Stanton what happened. We'll tell security. We can even tell the Wellington cops, too. We'll get your stuff back. Okay?"

"No, you don't get it," Carli whispered. "My real identity is all over the stuff that got stolen. Miranda wants to report it to the cops. If I were in LA, living my normal life, I wouldn't care. The stuff can be replaced. But now . . . I don't know. What should I do?"

I didn't know either. I opened my mouth, then closed it, then opened it again.

The words I found myself saying a minute later sounded frighteningly like Dad's. "Well, you're here to learn to be bad, right? And obviously a demented criminal, or several, is on the loose. So you have to think like a criminal in order to catch the culprit."

She didn't respond.

"Hello?"

"Fun!" she shrieked. "You're not helping! Don't you get it? If they find the stuff that was stolen . . ." She paused.

"They won't. They haven't found Darcy yet, right?"

"I'm not even going to acknowledge that statement," she growled.

I nodded. "Good idea. Let's pretend I never said it. In fact, let's pretend that none of this ever, ever happened. We've done a pretty good job of pretending so far."

Carli

Fun really pissed me off sometimes. I don't know how he could joke around after the break-in. Especially since his own future was on the line. If anybody besides Nails discovered the truth about me, and who I really was, that I was an actress . . . But there was no need for paranoia, right? Fun was right. My stuff was gone, and it would probably be gone forever. Just like Darcy: here today, gone tomorrow. I shouldn't be mad; Fun used dumb jokes the same way he used graffiti—as a defense mechanism. No wonder he and Nails got along so well. Nails was a fountain of dumb jokes. The vandal and the deranged psychopath. Two criminals, happy as clams.

FUN

Nails blogged about the robbery that night. Well, kind of. I was getting worried.

> A.I.= Anonymous Intimacy = Artificial Intelligence = Anyone Interested?
>
> 9/26
>
> I like this so-called blogosphere. It puts me in that A.I. mood. It allows me to say things that I otherwise wouldn't say out loud, to share my innermost feelings and secrets with the general public. Best of all I can convince myself that people actually care what I have to say. It's my own little world, and I'm the boss of it. Hooray!
>
> So here is my pearl of wisdom for the evening: Hate is like crack, people. Sure, hate gives you that sweet, empowering rush, but it's when the high is over, you feel lousy and wrung out and you crave more. Not that I've smoked crack (at least, not that I remember) . . . I'm just saying: for those of you out there who hate Sheila Smith and Miranda Jenkins, it's time to detox. Give them their stuff back. Give us Darcy Novak back. Let

the hate go. You'll feel better. Maybe not right away, but down the road you will. Trust me. I'm not trying to be holier than thou. Aside from certain Biblical prophets, all my heroes are criminals and/or drug addicts. So I can relate. That's what's so great about the Bible. It gives us all these great archetypes. Somebody can be as "wise as Solomon" or as "wicked as Jezebel." That is all.

Current Mood: Funky

What I'm listening to: Funkytown

Album: Mouth to Mouth

Artist: Lipps, Inc.

****

Comments: 1

Nails, please turn off that goddamn music, stop typing, and let me sleep.

—FUN

Carli

The cops arrived at around 3 A.M. to inspect our room, but there wasn't much they could do. There was a dearth of clues. No fingerprints, no dirt tracked in from outside. Whoever had stolen our stuff had worn gloves or wiped the place down. Lieutenant Jacobs, the particularly obese cop who in charge of the Darcy Novak investigation, seemed annoyed even to be awake.

"Compared to a missing girl, this is small potatoes," he said, yawning.

"I know!" I snapped. "But maybe these two crimes are related.

Maybe you could factor that in to your police report. If it isn't too much trouble."

"Leave the police work to me, miss. Stick to acting."

My jaw dropped. I turned to Miranda. She was speechless too. I snatched up my phone and dialed Stanton as the cops sauntered out of the room. I shouldn't have made the effort. He didn't care so much that we were robbed either. He told me "this [was] an internal school matter," that I "shouldn't have involved the police," and that "the last thing anybody [needed] was another scandal." He also assured me that they'd find our stolen stuff.

I felt more like Sheila Smith than ever before.

Fun

At lunch the following day, I broke down.

"Dude, did you kill Darcy?" I asked Nails again, in front of Carli and Miranda.

"Well, I'll tell you on one condition," Nails said, very calmly. "In my younger and more vulnerable years . . ." He paused. "I wasn't going anywhere with that." He frowned at us. "Kidding. It's the opening line of *The Great Gatsby*. And you wanted to be in the Book Society? Come on, Fun."

"What about a simpler question," Carli said. "Did you break into our room last night?"

"Not that I know of."

"How about this," Miranda put in. "Why'd you get kicked out of Hotchkiss?"

"I tried to smuggle opium out of Afghanistan."

Carli laughed. "Ha, ha."

"He's not joking," I muttered.

"You aren't?" Miranda and Carli gasped in unison.

"Fun makes it dound so stramatic," Nails said in a dismissive voice. "That's why I wound up here. My freshman roommate was this Afghani kid. Ahmed Al-Somebody, the son of a diplomat. And I was a pretty big stoner at the time. Ahmed was really shy and eager to please, so I talked him into bringing back some opium in a diplomatic pouch. He got caught."

"Nails, you know I'm really not in the mood for this," Carli moaned.

"I'm not kidding! I swear. The funny thing was, it happened midway through spring semester. Afterward, I was supposed to go to the local public high school in Greenwich. But they didn't have enough room for me. So my mom made me get a job. She didn't want me sitting around the house all day. That's when the trouble started."

"You are such a lying dog," Carli muttered.

Nails shrugged. "Interesting you say *dog*, Sheila. I had to take care of my neighbor's dog, Sunshine. She looked like a wolf. Her vet was this overweight fidgety lesbian. Not that the lesbian part matters, but she wasn't so nice. And after the eighth exam, she was like, 'Sunshine's fat and anxious.' She actually said those words, like it was a medical diagnosis. Besides, what *should* a wolflike dog be—calm? So, I was like, who are you? An anorexic Dalai Lama?"

Miranda's jaw dropped. "You *said* that?"

"No. I said 'Thanks, ma'am,' and left. But the point is, I thought it."

"So . . ." Miranda's crow's-feet darkened. "I don't get it. What trouble started?"

"I lied to my mom. I told her that Sunshine got a clean bill of health. Then I took her to the park the next day, and things got a little out of hand. Sunshine humped the swing set. But she was so fat and anxious that her heart gave out. She dropped dead. My mom sent me here as punishment."

I nodded, feeling sick. "That's a true story," I concurred.

Miranda laughed, her crow's-feet vanishing. "No it's not. Nails, everything you say is a lie. You can't fool me. I know it. Just like I know you didn't try to smuggle opium out of Afghanistan. Just like I know you had nothing to do with Darcy Novak or the robbery last night. Right?"

Carli

The second *Grease*-cast-and-crew-meets-Book Society meeting was understandably tense. Mr. Hines was late for some reason. A note was waiting for all of us too. It sat on the lacquered wooden table in the middle of the stuffy room, composed of different letters cut out from magazines—an M.O. ripped off from dozens of *Law & Order* episodes—pasted onto a sheet of notebook paper.

ONE OF YOU IS A PHONY, A LIAR, AND A THIEF!!

I wanted to ask everyone assembled (so far, Kirk, Mary, Peter, Lisa, and Miranda), Ever feel panicked and amused and disappointed, all at the same time? This was a hackneyed B-movie and straight-to-TV ploy. I'd probably seen half a dozen instances of it on any number of Dick Wolf shows, which was what freaked me out about it. Because I couldn't help but think, *This is meta. This is meant for someone who knows a lot about film and TV. This has all the hallmarks of Nails.*

Talk about creepy. As if stage-directed, Fun and Nails waltzed in moments later.

"Check *this* out," Miranda announced dramatically. She grabbed the psycho note off the table and shoved it into Nails's hands.

He studied it for a moment and shrugged. "I said pretty much the same thing on my blog the other night. It's been done." He tossed it to Fun.

Fun frowned as he sat down, his eyes flashing over the page again and again. He placed it back on the table. "That's weird," he said.

"That's the best you can come up with?" I demanded, my eyes on Nails.

"What do you want me to say?" Fun asked.

"You want to hear something really weird?" Nails asked. "My mom just sent me a check for forty-six dollars and eleven cents, along with a list of itemized deductions. She deducts the cost of my long-distance phone calls and utilities from my allowance. I'm supposed to get two hundred bucks a month, before expenses. God, I love that woman."

"I thought you hated your mom," Fun mumbled.

"Of course I hate her. But you can't hate somebody without loving that somebody first. The opposite of love is indifference." He jerked his head toward Kirk. "You think I give a crap about *him*? All I care about is getting Darcy back."

Kirk laughed. He scratched at his acne. "You know Nails, I don't think I ever thanked you properly for getting us the Book Society room. Once we get close to showtime, we can turn it into a private dressing room: flowers, scented candles . . ."

"Well, glad I could help. Speaking of doing other people's work for them, I also wrote Darcy's essay last year titled 'Epistemology: The Neary of Thollege.' Recently I've embarked on a career as a one-man private investigation unit, to make up for the cops."

I squirmed in my seat. My eyes drifted to the paper on the table, the paper nobody was talking about. Seeing as I'd been robbed two nights ago, and nobody had found my stuff, and Darcy was still missing—I decided to pick up the slack where Nails had left off on the investigative front.

Miranda chased after me. So did Nails. So did Fun.

For a second there, I was pretty pleased. I was too scared to be alone.

FUN

Outside in the cold, Carli kept quiet.

I tried to make up for her silence. I jabbered with Miranda and Nails about who would have done such a thing. We knew the cut-out note couldn't have been meant for any of *us*. "It's not that big a deal," I said, "especially not at Winchester. Kids used to hold occult rituals in the abandoned vineyards during the sixties . . ." But then I lost steam, especially looking at Carli's distraught face. I thought about Darcy.

"None of those crazy nutcases ever *killed* anybody," Carli murmured.

I couldn't argue. *Was* that note somehow connected to Darcy?

As these thoughts swirled, Miranda and Nails started talking again. Within seconds, they were off on a tangent, theorizing about the motives of psychopaths. Before long, they were looking into each other's eyes and finishing each other's sentences. Then all of a sudden, Nails offered to escort Miranda back to her dorm.

She agreed. The entire conversation took less than a minute and a half. I gaped at the two of them as they scampered off into the darkness. I hoped Carli was thinking the same thing I was. But then, any butt-wipe could guess what I was thinking.

What's going on with those two?

Carli

Honestly, I barely remember the next few days. I stopped sleeping. A gauzy fog enveloped me at all times, buffering me from focusing on Darcy. But I did notice weird little details, the way Fun would.

I noticed Miranda and Nails disappearing for long walks. I

noticed those tubby Wellington cops laughing about the cut-out letter, as if it too was a waste of their time. I noticed that I could actually survive without certain (stolen) amenities, such as a hair dryer and iPod. And I noticed Kirk requesting—right in front of me—that Mr. Hines give Mary Fishman my role as Sandy in *Grease.* I didn't have the energy or clarity to protest, but luckily Mr. Hines refused. Maybe I was out of it, but I could *sing.*

The icing on the proverbial cake? There was another cut-out note waiting for us at the next *Grease* and Book Society meeting. This time, Mr. Hines saw it.

Unsettling, to say the least.

I mean: Duh. *I* wasn't who I claimed to be. And Fun was in

cahoots with me. Which made him just as guilty.

Fun

The first thing I noticed at that third meeting:

All the books had been rearranged. They were shelved in a different order. I could tell by the color of the spines. At first I didn't see the reshelving as sinister, just weird. Yes, this was what life had come to: obsessing about the order of books in a room that reeked of garlic, as I tried to figure out the identity of a killer, kidnapper, or kleptomaniac—or combination.

Mr. Hines dismissed the cut-out notes as "a third-rate literary gag."

He didn't mention the reshelving. But he did tell us that the Book Society would be dissolved after one final "official" meeting, during which we would discuss *The Human Stain.* It was clearly counterproductive. I agreed. I'd forgotten why we were even there, in no small part because he'd brought his two children, both of whom weren't wearing shirts.

Carli

The following day at lunch, I caught myself staring across the cafeteria at Kirk, Sarah, and Mary. They were all wearing black. It seemed Sarah had given up playing the professional journalist. She'd gone back to being a Goth DJ. Had she given up on Darcy, too? Like the cops and Stanton had?

"What's Mary always writing in her notebook, anyway?" I whispered to Fun. "I mean, really?

"It's a diary. I peeked over her shoulder at the last Book Society meeting. She wrote about how she wants to re-audition for the role of Sandy by singing a song she 'wrote' by Pink Floyd. Her handwriting is pretty sloppy."

"She wrote that?" I asked.

"Yeah. Why?"

"She stole that from the movie *The Squid and the Whale.* There's this scene where the older son wins a school music contest for performing a . . . ah, forget it."

"So what are you saying?" Fun asked. "She's a thief and a liar? That she'll get caught? That she isn't who she claims to be?"

"All of the above. And she's in this room right now. Ha!"

Fun tried to smile, but he couldn't. It was a bad joke. I just wanted him to feel better. Oh—and one last thing: Miranda and I never got our stuff back. I don't know if the cops even bothered to look for it.

Fun

That night, Nails posted his final blog:

> What is love?
>
> 10.2
>
> Love is guilt, two sides of the same coin. Or maybe a better analogy would be pool balls. Love's a stripe; guilt's a solid. Pool has been on my mind a lot recently, and I'll tell you why: At the conclusion of the last Book Society meeting, Kirk Bishop waxed metaphorical on our way out the door. He said that every relationship is like a pool game. There's the initial break, the first meeting, where everything is in flux, but then the balls come to a standstill. And after that, the relationship-er

sees the relationship-ee as an opponent. Their qualities and flaws are the balls: You either want to keep them on the table or sink them. The trick is to size up the table from a distance, and not to get too hyped up. Prey on the weakness; capitalize on the strengths. Sink 'em or keep 'em on the table. Of course, he also said that he wanted to throw an "ugly sweater party" in honor of Miranda. I think he was trying to be funny. But speaking of not being funny and weakness and strength, have any of you seen that old show from the seventies, *The Six Million Dollar Man*, starring Lee Majors? Sheila Smith, I know you have, so this is going out to you. Isn't it weird how that show used slow motion to convey speed? How they used weakness to convey strength? And we viewers bought it. So what does that tell us? Maybe it levels the pool table? Maybe somebody who seems weak could be strong?

Current Mood: Not-so-funny

What I'm listening to: Bad Company

Album: Bad Company

Artist: Bad Company

****

Comments: 1

They used the same trick in the movie *Wolf*, starring Jack Nicholson and James Spader—slow motion to convey speed. I think it's time we all moved faster.

—Sheila Smith

4 The Book Society meets for the very last time, whereupon Fun makes an extremely upsetting discovery.

Carli

To say that I was dreading that last official meeting of the Book Society gives far too much justice to the word *dread*.

I decided to bring my laptop, just in case I need to e-mail Dr. Fein or Grizz. I had an awful feeling, a premonition. I knew there would be another nasty surprise waiting for us. Yes, even nastier than the psychotic cut-out notes. (On the glass-half-full side, at least those notes might keep us from talking about *The Human Stain,* which I still hadn't finished.) The premonition had to do with the movie *Get Shorty.*

I'd watched the movie on my laptop the night before; it was

my only solace from the sleeplessness. Anyway, there's a scene where an old mob boss climbs a darkened staircase. It's right at the beginning. Fun and I had to climb a very similar staircase to get to the private little room where we meet in the library, even though we had to climb down instead of up . . . and . . . ah, forget it. It sure bored Fun when I tried to explain it to him.

"I'm sorry, what?" he asked, his footsteps creaking in the shadows behind me.

"You have an annoying habit of tuning me out," I whispered.

"I'm sorry, what?" he repeated, chuckling.

"Ha, ha."

On the Annoying-Habit-O-Meter, Fun's sense of humor ranked quite high, somewhere above his habit of staring at his own paintings and slightly below his habit of wearing a new ZZ Top concert T-shirt (I mean, *ZZ Top*?). He only wears it because he thinks he's making an anti-Winchester statement. Nobody deigns to listen to "classic rock." And maybe it *is* a statement, but nobody notices. Everybody is too self-involved. Which I guess actually makes it sort of cute, not that I'd ever tell him—okay, I'm rambling again. You want naughty? I'll give you naughty. The shirt is hideous, and ZZ Top bites. They're even worse than Iron Maiden. There. I said it.

I paused at the bottom of the stairs. "Hey, Fun, can I ask you something?"

"What, you want me to change T-shirts?"

"No. Well, I mean, *yes*, I do, but I want to ask you about Miranda."

"What about her?"

"She seems to be ignoring the fact that Nails has completely lost his mind," I whispered. "She still won't stop talking about him."

Fun wasn't smiling anymore. Right then, my heart squeezed. He had a crush on her. Of course he did. He just wouldn't admit it. He was still trying to get over Charity Barker. It's a natural reaction: You try to get over somebody by falling for a stranger. And it's always the same old problem. Crushes come on fast. Yes, I speak from personal experience. Dr. Fein can attest to this. I'd thought Fun was cute from day one, and I didn't want to admit that, either. I hadn't fully, until now.

"You do like Miranda, don't you?" I asked. "I'm sorry."

"Actually, no. I wasn't even thinking about her."

"You weren't?"

"No. I was thinking about that poem Nails wrote, and about Stanton's speech on the radio the day Darcy disappeared, and about what Kirk told me out in the woods."

I frowned. "What do you mean?"

"Nails might be right. I really don't think any of this has to do with Darcy . . . I mean, not personally. I think it has to do with money. Listen." He plopped down on the steps. "I know this will sound crazy, but I think maybe Stanton *did* kidnap her. He's making it seem like there's a psycho on the loose. That would explain the break-in, too, and the notes, and the fact that he's sitting on his butt about it all. Ten to one, in the next few days, he'll discover a ransom note. Once someone pays up, he'll spring Darcy, find your stuff, and look like the hero—and then pin the blame on someone else." He bit his lip, for once looking as if he'd regretted what he'd said. "Like Nails."

I shrugged. "You know what?

"What?"

"From what I've seen of this school, it doesn't sound crazy at all. Anything is possible, Fun. Anything."

Fun

Carli was pretty adept at using her laptop: another hidden talent. I imagined she'd hunt and peck rather than touch-type. It didn't even matter that the stairwell was so dark.

"All right, so we know he's 'E Stanton' at winchesterarts-dot-edu," she breathed, her fingers clattering. Her face glowed blue in the light of the screen. "What do you think his password is?"

I thought for a second. Stanton was definitely not the most original guy in the world. Well, unless he *was* an arch criminal. "Try his wife's name. Eliza."

"Eliza," she repeated slowly. She typed it in and hit ENTER. "Bingo."

"Really? Damn. This place *is* low-security."

"Where should we start?"

I peered over Carli's shoulder at his list of e-mails. The oldest read DRAFT OF DARCY SPEECH. It had been sent to his private e-mail address. My eyes sped over the words and all those little instructions to himself . . . *Jesus.* Most of the other e-mails were about money. Pleas to the Bishop family to maintain the Nicholas Barrington Center for Theater and Arts. Pleas to the Novak family to relax and just send in that tuition deposit; Darcy would turn up sooner or later. "Darcy might have even found an agent!" he wrote—as if that would somehow reassure them.

My God, I remember thinking. *For once in his life, Kirk Bishop isn't full of it.*

Carli

"Karmaggedon," Fun breathed.

"Indeed," I whispered back. I snapped shut the laptop and shoved it back into its case. We hurried down the stairs. The other members of the Book Society were already present, sitting around the table: Kirk, Mary, Sarah, Miranda, and Nails. Everybody looked exhausted. They glared at us as Fun shut the door. Nobody made a peep.

"Want to explain *this*?" Mary barked, waving a piece of notebook paper at me.

I gasped.

Spelled out in those same poorly cut, glossy magazine letters was:

"You're the one who made the alphabet soup," Kirk said. He wrinkled his beaklike nose. "Trying to keep your enemies close and your friends closer, eh?"

"Is that a quote from *The Human Stain*?" Fun asked.

Actually, it was a quote from *The Godfather.* Or rather, in typical Kirk Bishop fashion, he misquoted. The real quote goes: "Keep your *friends* close but your *enemies* closer." But I was a little too upset to smile. I wasn't trying to keep anyone close. He hadn't even thanked me for the soup. Nobody had, except Fun and Nails and Miranda.

"Who *are* you, anyway?" Kirk demanded. He sat up straight, his beady little eyes darting back and forth between Fun and me. "I mean, I know you're a transfer, Sheila . . . but from where? And why do you and Fun always do everything together? Did you know each other before? I know most of the families associated with this school."

Uh-oh times two. This was bad. It wasn't only bad because we were in danger of blowing the whole *Private Nights* fraud, but also because, thanks to some clever sociopath, suddenly *we* were the prime suspects for all this craziness. I glanced at Fun. For a second, I thought he was going to just come right out and confess. That I'd been sent here under false pretenses because of some dumb TV show, and Fun was assigned to "assist" me, and the whole thing was an act, and blah, blah, blah.

Incidentally, Dr. Fein's last text message went:

"Carli, given the rambling nature of your past few messages, and the cloying wish-you-were-here's, it's clear you can't handle the stress of this 'Sheila' business. I think I should come get you or you should come home." Ha! She wasn't the only one.

I did what I always do when I can't handle the stress. I started rambling. "You guys, I swear to God, I've never stolen anything in my life! And Fun just felt sorry for me because I'm a transfer, and I don't know . . . and that's probably why Nails and Miranda hooked up too—I mean, not to embarrass you, Miranda, like it's not *bad* that you did hook up . . ." I tried to laugh. It didn't work.

"I know you're not involved in any wrongdoing, Sheila," Miranda said out of nowhere. "I don't know who it is, but it's definitely not you."

The room fell silent. I studied Miranda.

The freakiest part of all? *I* knew she was lying.

See, one of the things I've learned from movies (specifically *House of Games*, starring Lindsay Crouse and Joe Mantegna, and *True Romance*, starring Christian Slater and Patricia Arquette) is that everybody has a "tell," or "pantomime," a nervous little twitch people make when they're hiding something. I'd proved it in fact, with my mind-reading gag, a magic trick I used to play on my friends back home.

The mind-reading gag works like this: You give someone a coin. You ask them to hide it in either of their fists. Then you tell them to hold both fists out. And as they're standing there, both fists in front of them, you say a lot of hocus-pocus-type gibberish to distract them. Meanwhile, you're secretly watching out for their "tell," a little glance toward the coin, a slight movement, something they don't even realize they're doing—and, *presto*—you know which fist the coin is in.

To them, though, it seems as if you're reading their mind.

Anyway, Miranda was adjusting the little handwoven friendship bracelet on her left wrist, sliding it up her arm so that it wouldn't hang loose. Not a big deal at first look, right? But that's the "tell." I knew she only adjusted her bracelet when she was being deceptive. She did it when I asked her if she liked old Katharine Hepburn movies, because I had a bunch on DVD. (*"Sure,* Bringing up Baby . . . *great!"*) She did it when she agreed enthusiastically to a makeover. (*"Yes, I'd love one! Just not right this second!")* She did it when she denied liking Nails. And she was doing it now.

The question, of course, remained: What was she lying about?

I saw her steal a surreptitious peek at Nails. Another "tell."

It took every ounce of self-control I had not to gape at him the same way everybody was gaping at me. *I bet Miranda DOES know who broke into our room! I bet it's Nails! We knew it all along! She's lying to protect him, because she's so head-over-heels in love and can't keep her hands off him! It's so evil and rotten!*

But it was also really sort of sweet, if you think about it.

Fun

For the first time, I pitied Carli. It could have been a turning point in our relationship, I guess. I don't know. Obsessing over psychological stuff like that is her area of expertise, not mine. I stick to the details. And sure, I'd felt a little bad for her before. All her good intentions seemed to backfire and blow up in her face. But the way these jerks were accusing her now, these jerks I'd known for years . . . It was wrong. Her own roommate had vouched for her innocence. And in spite of this pure and brave vouching, Kirk and Sarah and Mary *still* didn't believe Carli.

About five seconds passed—everybody staring at each other with their mouths hanging open like lobotomy patients—before Kirk lit into Carli again.

"Why did you confess, Sheila?" he asked. "Are you living a double life? Like the life Coleman Silk led in *The Human Stain?*"

I longed for a paint can. Then I could spray an obscenity on Kirk and stuff the can in his mouth and photograph it. And in awe, some artistic foundation would present me a grant to attend the college of my choice.

"I didn't confess anything," Carli said, twittering anxiously.

"Sheila?" I said. "Are you okay?"

"I'm fine. I have nothing to confess. I swear to God I only prepared the alphabet soup for everyone as a polite gesture. I wanted to lighten things up a bit, make things less formal and more fun, and I already admitted that I haven't read the book. Look, I may not be perfect, but I try not to lie whenever possible . . ."

Oh boy. I tuned out. This was too painful. Being the person she is, she'd missed out on one of life's crucial lessons: *Get yourself off the hook.* Big problem. She'd always put herself *on* the hook: volunteering, cooking soup for jerks, taking responsibility for herself, the rest of it. So, naturally, when she was accused of something, even something false, she had no idea how to react. She flipped.

I, on the other hand, was an expert at getting myself off the hook. Well, sort of an expert. Okay, I wasn't an expert at all. If I were an expert at getting myself off the hook, then I wouldn't be babysitting Carli, a.k.a. Sheila Smith, in the first place. But I stayed cool in the face of doom, at least. Or I tried to.

The real psycho would be caught. I knew, because he had screwed up with this lame "Alphabet Soup" note. I'd had a grudging respect for whoever it was until now. Some crooked genius who could kidnap a student, rearrange the bookshelves, cut out letters from magazines, and manage to steal tons of stuff, all while staying anonymous. But implicating Carli? No. Not so bright. The girl is incapable of doing anything wrong. Spend thirty seconds with her, and you'd figure that out.

So while Carli continued to plead, and all the rest of them kept hurling accusations at her—except Nails and Miranda, seeing as they'd had nothing to do with it, either—I began to wonder: Why *would* such a smart person make such a dumb mistake? And that led me to consider something.

Maybe it was deliberate. Maybe the note didn't refer to Carli, after all. Maybe it referred to the actual *alphabet*. Because, as Kirk had rightly mentioned the first time the books had been rearranged, the shelves in this room were no longer filed alphabetically according to author. They were, however, filed in the exactly same pattern as they had been at the previous meeting, and the one before that. I knew this for certain, because the pattern of the colors of the book spines had stuck in my head. (Color patterns tend to do that.) The pattern was probably something all of these pseudo-intellectual, self-proclaimed literati should have noticed but failed to.

Or maybe one of them didn't *want* others to notice . . . until the time was right. Maybe somebody had cooked up a *symbolic* alphabet soup by rearranging the books.

A long shot, sure, but whatever.

I turned to the shelves.

Even though we were supposed to meet to discuss one of the more recent works of Philip Roth, or at least the lines from *Grease,* this little room was dedicated entirely to science fiction: Isaac ***A***simov, Ray ***B***radbury, Arthur C. ***C***larke, Philip K. ***D***ick, and so on. When arranged alphabetically, that is.

So I decided to conduct a little experiment. I took the first letter of the author's last name of the first book on the left of the top shelf: *Shadows over Innsmouth*, by Stephen ***J***ones. I did this because another Stephen Jones book was also first to the left on the shelf below—and *another* book of his was first to the left on the left below that. And the first book below *that* was *Divine Endurance*, by Gwyneth ***J***ones.

My breath came fast.

My eyes flashed compulsively left to right, left to right, again and again. The pattern repeated on every shelf: Books by the same author—or at least an author whose last name began with same letter—filed in the exact same order, shelf by shelf.

Those letters spelled a message.

JAMES HILTON FROM QUEENS IS HILTON JAMES

On every single shelf.

Ray Bradbury's books were gone. He's a B name, and B wasn't

part of the message. So were Arthur C. Clarke's books, for the same reason. So were Philip K. Dick's books. Obviously. I didn't really care about the missing books. Science fiction bites, as far as I'm concerned. No, the worst of it was that I'd been wrong. The perpetrators hadn't made a mistake at all. They *were* smart, smarter than either Carli or I had imagined. And whoever they were, they had just implicated my best friend—

"Fun?" Carli asked.

"Yeah?"

"Would you mind walking me back to my room? I've had enough. *I* was robbed."

"I know," I said.

I turned and threw the door open, ignoring all the self-righteous glowering faces.

I tried to ignore Nails's face too. He was staring at me with an expression I knew very well, one he'd given me a dozen times in similar circumstances, back when Darcy was still around . . . the one that asked, *Why are you leaving me alone with all these schmucks?*

I didn't feel so bad for Carli anymore. I felt a lot worse for me. But at least that was a familiar feeling. Familiarity is always comforting.

5 Fun and Carli begin and conclude their investigation—in earnest.

Carli

That night, way past lights-out, I met Fun in the vineyards at his request. He wanted to talk alone in a secluded location. I admit a part of me was excited. Sneaking out after curfew was naughty. Even more naughty than breaking into Darcy's room. Even more naughty than what Nails was probably doing right now with Miranda. Well, not really. But as I crawled through the prickly branches—breaking some as I went, snapping others behind me like whips—the excitement faded. It was freezing cold. My arms and face were lacerated. And if we got caught, Fun would be expelled, and so would I, and we'd never find out what happened to Darcy.

"Over here!" a voice hissed at me.

I followed the sound, scrambling through the brush by a tiny clearing next to the abandoned distillery. Again, disappointment washed over me. I'd ventured near the distillery a few times before during my brief tenure at Winchester, and I'd heard all the rumors (mostly that kids kept making wine here until the late eighties), but I'd never actually laid eyes on it. I don't know—I was expecting some sort of wondrous Charlie-and-the-Chocolate-Factory-style fairy-tale palace.

It really wasn't much more than a broken-down shack. Several chimneys jutted from a sloped roof. The sky was clear and the moon was bright, so I could see that all the windows were either cracked or missing. Fun paced beside the door, bundled up in a sweatshirt-on-sweatshirt, knit-cap combo. His breath made frosty little clouds.

"So, what do you think?" he whispered.

I shrugged, staring at the distillery door. It was rotted in several places, barely hanging on the hinges. Haphazardly spray-painted on it were the words: WE SELL NO WINE BEFORE ITS TIME—ERNEST AND JULIO WINCHESTER.

"I don't know. Is that your work?"

Fun frowned. "Carli, I'm serious. What do you think that that hidden message on the bookshelf means? Do you think somebody is trying to frame Nails?"

I shook my head. "I don't know. You're in a better position to say than I am. You actually know the guy."

"You know him too," Fun shot back. "You *like* him."

"No, I don't!" I answered automatically. "I mean, not like

that. Yuck." I wrapped my arms around myself, staring up at the night sky. It was pretty amazing how many stars you could see out here, when the sky was clear. In LA, you could hardly see any. "What do you think we should do?"

He leaned against the distillery wall, looking very tired in the moonlight. "Maybe we should just call my father and get you home, and get the cops involved for real. Because this thing is way over my head."

I stepped closer to him. "Are you telling me to run away?"

"No! But—"

"Fun, you've seen the cops. What could they possibly do to help? Besides, your dad would be on my side. The whole point of this *Private Nights* venture is to soak up sexy boarding-school realism, right? Although now it's two lonely underdogs, trying to find the missing starlet? What's that? Like, *The Outsiders* meets *LA Confidential*?"

He laughed quietly. "Right. With Harry-Met-Sally heart."

"Come on," I murmured. "If you send me home, you'll probably lose your trust fund, yada, yada, yada . . . It's up to *us* to figure out who the culprit is. Don't you get it?"

He turned away and exhaled, producing a ghostly, moonlit bluish-white cloud. It hung for a split second over his head. "I say we go through his e-mail again," he stated, his back still turned to me. "Or at least Google him or something. I don't care about 'wrongdoing.' And please stop using that word. It's lame. The point is, if you are gonna stay, you can't keep me from getting in trouble. Understood?"

I nodded, my eyes on the graffiti-stained door. "Understood," I repeated.

* * *

FUN

We went to Carli's room. Miranda had apparently snuck out to be with Nails. Lucky him. He was cuddling (or worse) with a gorgeous-if-freakish senior transfer. And here I was, also with a gorgeous-if-freakish senior transfer . . . only I wasn't cuddling, and even if *he* wasn't, he was breaking the rules with a girl in a much more enjoyable way.

"Google 'Hilton James New York,'" Carli muttered into my ear. She leaned over the desk chair, shifting from foot to foot, staring at her computer screen, one pigtail brushing against my cheek. "If there are any newspaper articles, I'd search those first."

"I will. Would you just . . . mind not hovering?"

"No problem," she said. She retreated into the shadows.

Carli's room smelled. It would be rude to tell her, but it did.

It smelled like stale sheets, or—dare I say it? No, I wouldn't. I wouldn't sink to Nails's level to make a dumb crack about the Winchester laundry. I clicked, and about three zillion articles popped up, as I knew they would. (Though for some reason, several were in German.) Most of the closest matches were either prints or reprints of the same two obituaries.

New York Times

OCTOBER 4, 2000

Greenwich boy killed in car crash

HILTON JAMES, aged 10, died from complications due to injuries resulting from an automobile accident on the Merritt Parkway today. A private service will be held at St. Mary's Episcopal Church. Mourners are asked to donate to the local soccer league . . . (FOR FULL ACCESS TO THIS ARTICLE, SUBSCRIBE TO THE NYTIMES ONLINE TODAY.)

New York Times

DECEMBER 2, 2000

Queens orphan given new life

In a rags-to-riches story that could be torn straight from the pages of a modern-day Charles Dickens novel, 10-year-old James Hilton, an only child whose single mother tragically passed away this month due to complications from lung cancer, was . . . . (FOR FULL ACCESS TO THIS ARTICLE, SUBSCRIBE TO THE NYTIMES ONLINE TODAY.)

"What the hell do you think this means?" I whispered.

"I can guess," Carli said, hovering over my chair again. "I can guess it means that James Hilton from Queens took over Hilton James's identity. I wouldn't be surprised if he wants to ride the phony pedigree all the way to the top of some sick heap. You think Kirk Bishop is bad? I'll bet you Nails is about a million times worse than Kirk Bishop. 'Nails' is an apt nickname. He's a probably a sociopath—"

"Carli, relax," I interrupted.

She retreated to her bed. "Sorry. I'm upset."

"So am I. But do you really believe that Nails is worse than Kirk Bishop? This guy has been my best friend for more than *two years*. Yes, there have always been some puzzling anomalies, as far as he goes. His accent, the fact that I've only been invited to his home once—even though Greenwich is a lot closer than LA—but there's no way . . . Is there?" I spun around in her desk chair and stared at her.

She scrunched the bed sheets with her clammy hands. "Well, we have other suspects," she said. "I mean, other suspects in terms of the whole robbery thing. There's Kirk. Maybe he didn't really like Darcy all that much. And then there's Sarah. Maybe she's gone crazy too. You were the one who told me that she never wore pantsuits."

I rubbed my eyes. "I guess," I croaked. I sounded like an old man. I felt like one. My best friend was a fraud, and so was I, even though I didn't have any wrinkles (yet) and wasn't a convict (yet). "Let's go to bed."

"Excuse me?" Carli asked with a laugh.

"Let's go to bed," I repeated, yawning.

"What? You mean you, with me, now?"

"No! I mean . . . you know what I mean."

She laughed and stood. "I'm teasing you. Not to get all 'meta' on you or anything, but people tend to hook up at times when they're most stressed. It's a device guys like your dad use in every sitcom and B movie ever created. Every psych course, too. Speaking of which, I need to check in with my shrink. So get out of my chair."

I obeyed. I'd never heard her dish out commands. I wasn't sure if I was frightened or flabbergasted or, well . . . no need to go there.

Carli shoved me aside and clicked on her e-mail.

I hovered over her shoulder, as she'd hovered over mine, watching as she accessed her only unread message, from an untraceable source:

> WE KNOW WHO YOU ARE. YOU ARE CARLI GEMZ. WE SAW YOU IN A SKITTLES COMMERCIAL. IF YOU DON'T TELL EVERYONE AT WINCHESTER THE TRUTH TOMORROW, WE WILL MAKE SURE YOUR CAREER IS RUINED. YOU DON'T BELONG HERE. GET OUT.
> P.S. WE ALSO THINK YOU'RE THE THIEF AND THE KIDNAPPER.

Well. What a pleasant surprise. Carli's cover was blown. And she was *still* a suspect. I didn't bother saying anything. What was the point? Carli trembled at her desk as if she'd come down with a cold, which I knew she hadn't, because she'd told me she never got sick. We left without a word. We didn't even bother closing the door behind us. Besides, there was nothing of value to steal, other than her computer.

Carli

My vision wouldn't clear no matter how furiously I blinked. The insomnia was finally catching up with me. (I wasn't even sure what time it was, maybe 2 A.M.?). No matter. We marched toward Bryant Manor, bent on confronting Nails. I wondered if we'd be caught. Doubtful. Mr. Hines wasn't doing such a bang-up job as head of Security. Who would have picked him for that job in the first place? He was a balding, divorced, drama instructor with two out-of-control, gnomelike children. He never gave a crap about securing *them.* How could he be responsible for more than three hundred teenagers?

When we threw open the door and stormed upstairs to Fun's room . . .

My vision suddenly sharpened. In that instant I understood the meaning of *petrified*: being so scared that you literally freeze. I would have to remember this feeling if I were ever cast in a horror movie. If I survived, that is.

"Holy crap," Fun breathed.

The scene that greeted us was eerily familiar: a destroyed room. Nails wasn't home. But somebody had definitely been here, and it looked as if that somebody (maybe Nails himself?) had gone on a violent rampage. Books, clothes, and papers were strewn everywhere, Fun's desk had been overturned, Nails's computer was turned on—the keyboard was on the floor—and he seemed to have been interrupted in the middle of a paper. Even from the doorway, I could read the title on the screen, typed in bold caps:

TRUE PAIN FOR MY SHAM FRIENDS AND CHAMPAGNE FOR MY TRUE FRIENDS A HYPOCRISY OF STUDY IN U.S. POLITICS BY HILTON JAMES

"I think he meant 'study of hypocrisy,'" Fun whispered.

Somebody tapped my shoulder from behind before I could answer.

I nearly fainted. I whirled around—and was face to face with that old, familiar roommate of mine, Miranda Jenkins.

She raised a finger to her lips with one hand, indicating silence. In her other hand, she held a pistol. Interestingly, I recognized the model. Last May I'd auditioned for a pilot (Oliver Stone was rumored to be on the verge of signing on as an executive producer) about young undercover female cops. The show was called *WHUP-ass*. I forget what WHUP stood for; it was an acronym. The show never got past the second script reading. But I did have to handle a gun for the first time in my life. And it was the exact same: a nine-millimeter Glock. I remember being surprised at how heavy it was, even though it was only pretend-loaded.

I could only imagine how heavy Miranda's was.

She ushered us into the room and closed the door behind us.

"Don't worry," she said under her breath. "I'm a private investigator."

FUN

I laughed. That's the God's honest truth. I privately vowed right then and there that if I lived to see the dawn, I would call Carli's shrink and have her recommend a therapist for me. The hysterics began in fitful little giggles, and before I knew it, I was stomping my feet and howling. Stress has a funny effect on people.

"Shut up!" Miranda hissed.

I chomped down hard on my cheek. It worked.

She tucked the gun in the back of her jeans and yanked a wallet out of her front pocket, flipping it open in that exact same way cop characters flipped theirs open on TV. Sure enough, it revealed a badge: silver, Israeli-flag-shaped, a little nicked and rusted, embossed with MIRANDA JENKINS, PRIVATE INVESTIGATOR. It looked like a gag prize at a county fair. But what really caught my attention was the driver's license beneath it. According to the birth date, she was twenty-four years old.

"Who the hell *are* you?" I demanded.

"I told you, a P.I."

"But what are you doing *here*?"

"Who *are* you?" Carli snapped.

Miranda sighed. "Listen, up until four months ago, I was a cop in Stamford, Connecticut, all right? I made detective pretty fast, and since I have these babyish looks, I was given a lot of undercover work. I learned pretty fast that you make a lot more cash if you go into business for yourself. So I quit the force and became a P.I. But by the way, my boyfriend *is* a twenty-two-year-old gym teacher, and we did do it in the girls' locker room once. My training officer said I should tell the truth whenever I can."

Carli's complexion turned as white as Nails's. "Sounds like acting."

"It *is* acting," Miranda said with a shrug.

"So are you here because of Darcy Novak?" I pressed.

Miranda nodded. "Her parents hired me in August to keep an eye on her this semester. She'd received some threatening letters over the summer, warning her not to return to school—Hey, mind if I sit?"

I shook my head, unable to speak. Three minutes ago, I would have described Miranda Jenkins as a semi-hot nineteen-year-old senior transfer that I might possibly have a crush on. Now she was this . . . this . . . *grown-up*. I was suddenly repulsed. I jerked my chin toward the overturned chair next to my desk.

"Thanks." Miranda lifted the chair and straddled it, backward. "See, I thought this would be an easy gig—rich screwup kids, bohemian boarding school . . . I was supposed to be a secret bodyguard. But when I *got* here, Darcy was already gone." Her eyes flashed to Carli. "I wasn't faking when you found me crying the first day of school. I was upset. I *liked* Darcy. I botched my first big case in the most tragic way possible."

"You think it's botched?" I asked with a sinking feeling.

"I do. I'm not hopeful. There hasn't been a ransom demand. There really isn't an upside to a disappearance with no ransom demand."

Hmm. Well, I could think of an upside. I didn't have so much of a crush on Miranda Jenkins anymore. None at all, in fact. Probably best not to mention that, though.

"So what's your plan?" Carli asked quietly.

"Well, when I saw those cut-out notes, I immediately thought a student was responsible." She glanced up at our blank faces.

"Oh, right. See, the threatening letters were sent like that too, to the Novaks, over the summer. And Nails seemed like the perfect candidate. He was her ex-boyfriend, a dumped one, no less, and, well . . ."

"Well, what?" I demanded.

"I don't know if I should tell you this . . ."

"Tell us!" Carli barked. "No more secrets or lies!"

"They have something on him. He isn't who he says he is. He's um . . . he's not Hilton James. He's . . . someone else."

"Yeah, yeah, we know: He's James Hilton of Queens," Carli said.

Miranda frowned. "How do *you* know that?"

"We looked it up online," I grumbled. "It took us three seconds."

"Oh." Miranda blinked. "Well, he's in trouble."

"He is?"

"I told Nails I was a P.I. the night after the second Book Society meeting. I figured he would get scared and confess. But after an interrogation, I knew—"

"Whoa, slow down," I cut in. "You *interrogated* him?"

"It wasn't some Abu G'raib scenario, although Nails kept shouting that it was," she muttered. "But he agreed to cooperate with my investigation. Our whole couple thing was an act. But now . . . well, now we have a new crisis on our hands."

I swallowed, feeling dizzy. I couldn't even look at Carli. "What's that?"

Miranda stood. "Fifteen minutes ago, I got a call from an

untraceable number. The caller disguised his voice. He said I needed to show him 'a modicum of respect' by stopping my investigation immediately and leaving school, or my snitch was going to pay with his life. What I'm saying is: the *real* culprit learned the truth and kidnapped Nails."

I shook my head. *Modicum of respect . . . modicum of respect . . .* That would be a nice thing to experience. Even though Nails was in danger, I was pretty pissed at him too. He was a total phony! We'd been best friends for over two freaking years! And why didn't he confide in me about who Miranda really was? I'd told him who *Carli* was.

"What are you thinking?' Carli asked.

"Kirk Bishop," I found myself blurting—and Miranda answered with the same name at the exact same time.

That word . . . that stupid SAT word: *modicum.*

Of course it was Kirk Bishop. But if he was indeed the culprit, what did he do with Nails? As I stared at Miranda, we both began to nod slowly. The answer came to us: Kirk would hold Nails in a place so obvious that no smart person would ever think to look there, the one place nobody ever wanted to go, the very room Nails had secured: In the library basement, where the Book Society and *Grease* cast used to meet.

Carli

The room was empty.

I don't know what I was expecting. Maybe I was just hoping Fun and Miranda would be right. It was four in the morning and I was frazzled. For a while, the three of us just stood there—Miranda with her gun drawn—gazing at the empty chairs and bookshelves. Maybe the books were in proper order this time, maybe not. It didn't seem to matter. I was starting to think that Fun and I should just go to sleep and leave the detective work to the real detective.

But as we languished in growing disappointment and growing panic over the fate of Nails and Darcy, I heard a little sound over the hum of the ceiling fan, a little *clink, clink*, like marbles rattling around in a can, followed by a long hiss.

Fun's eyes bulged. "Listen!" he whispered.

Miranda and I shrugged at each other.

"Don't you get it? It's the sound of somebody spray-painting." He shook his head, his jaw twitching. "This is messed up. This is bad. Nobody at this school does graffiti but *me*." He marched out the door.

"Fun, wait—"

Miranda clamped a hand over my mouth. The three of us snaked our way through a near pitch-black labyrinth of corridors, drawing closer and closer to the sound . . . and to a flickering light, almost like a flame, casting grotesque shadows on the wall.

My heart thumped. Loudly. I was worried the sound might give us up. That, or I was on the verge of having a deadly coronary. I hadn't signed on for this when I agreed to soak up the "bona fides" of a prep school. It was not in my contract. The words of Dr. Fein's last e-mail echoed through my mind: *Carli, as a former child star I know how tempting it can be to confuse fantasy and reality, but ask yourself: Is there anything about your current life that is real right now?* Yes, Dr. Fein. And it was a little *too* real. What I'd give to be back in LA.

At the end of the hall, Miranda seized Fun's shoulder.

He straightened and froze. She moved ahead of him and raised her gun, lifting her finger to her lips as she'd done back outside his room.

Crouching low in the darkness, I ducked behind Miranda and peered around the corner, and for the first time ever in my life, I had to bite my lip to keep from screaming. Nails was sitting on the floor, still in that same stinky T-shirt. Only now his legs were tied with rope, and his hands were bound behind his back, and his mouth was gagged with a strip of duct tape, and his eyes were wide with fear. (His spiky hair seemed to have collapsed a bit too.) And Kirk Bishop stood over him, spray-painting something on the wall by the light of a candle . . .

I had to squint to make it out.

I fell on the floor in disbelief. It read:

I'M FUN AND I LOVE

FUN

"Kirk, what the hell are you *doing*?" I barked, unable to control myself.

He turned and glared at the three of us. His eyes honed in on the gun.

"I'm tagging," he said.

I forgot to be scared there for a second, mostly out of confusion.

Kirk took the opportunity to hurl the paint can at us. He dropped the candle and took off into the darkness.

"Stay here!" Miranda growled. She reached into her back pocket, dug out a penlight, and tossed it at us—then dashed after Kirk.

Carli and I looked at each other. Then we looked at Nails. He groaned furiously, his eyes dilated. We dropped to the cold cement floor and untied him as fast as we could, jabbing through the duct tape with the penlight until we'd shredded it.

"Ouch!" Nails gasped, once we tore the tape off his mouth.

"Sorry," Carli muttered.

"Are you okay?" I asked.

"No!" he shouted, his voice hoarse. He stood and kicked the pile of tape and rope against the wall. "I was freaking kidnapped! By Kirk and Mary!"

Carli and I turned to each other. "Mary?" we both said.

"Yeah, Mary."

"Why?" Carli asked breathlessly.

"How the hell should I know? She mentioned something about the distillery. She wanted to raise a toast to vanquishing her enemies. She . . ."

Nails kept jabbering as the three of us hurtled toward the stairs. Nails was alive; that was all we needed to know. Darcy was still a big, fat question mark.

* * *

Carli

On the inside, the distillery wasn't so bad. It was much nicer than its decrepit shell would suggest, with the graffiti on the door and whatnot. The floors were pretty much still intact. Even better, the stairs down to the well were too. I prayed and prayed and prayed, squeezing Fun's hand as we clambered down into the black abyss and dropped into the cramped cell. The penlight's narrow beam bounced over the damp stone walls. *Please let her be alive. Please let her be alive . . .*

"There!" Nails croaked.

He was right. After a frantic three-second search we found Darcy Novak. She sat in the middle of the floor, bound and gagged just as Nails had been: same rope, same duct tape, same horrified look. Here she was: alive and breathing, the girl who'd haunted me ever since I'd arrived at this nuthouse.

I ripped the duct tape off her mouth.

"Ouch," she gasped.

Yes, we'd disobeyed Miranda's order to stay put.

Darcy was filthy; she smelled like a locker room; she needed to brush her teeth; she was rail thin. But she was the most beautiful girl I'd ever seen. She looked sort of like Heather Graham, but shorter. Nails leaped over me and tore off the rest of her bonds, sweeping her into his arms. She hugged him back, sobbing. I stared at the floor. I shot a quick glance at Fun. He seemed choked up. I felt a lump forming in my own throat.

"What are you thinking?" Nails whispered.

Darcy smiled at us through her tears. "That I wish we had

a camera," she answered, and I knew at that moment she would make a better Sandy than I could ever possibly make. Her voice was so rich and musical, even with the dehydration. "Reunited and it feels so nice," she sang. "Reunited—"

"Reunited!" a voice cackled from the steps.

In the very first real movie I ever starred in, *Devil's Daughter,* a ski-masked, black-clad figure appeared at the penultimate moment. It wasn't a "real" movie; it was one of those cheesy made-for-Lifetime movies. (I played the daughter.) I was struck by how this figure's costume resembled that of the villain in that movie.

"What are you doing down here?" the figure asked.

I frowned. The voice belonged to a girl.

Nails and Fun glanced at each other. For a second, in spite of my fear, I felt a fleeting sense of empowerment. Apparently, Fun and Nails did too. Because without wasting a second, they both tackled the figure and ripped off the mask. *Holy crap.* It was Mary Fishman. She lay there on the cold, wet floor, pinned down by Fun, in the glare of the penlight. She and Fun were both hyperventilating.

"What in name's God is going on?" Nails demanded.

Mary bowed her head. "Nothing," she gasped.

Fun tightened his grip on her throat. "Don't lie."

"Ask Kirk!" Mary shrieked. "Kirk! I love—"

"Shut up," Nails snapped. Fun let go of her. He turned to me. I turned to Darcy. She raised her shoulders.

"Winchester—it's, like, a sick place to begin with. All sorts of plans are hatched every day here, right?" Mary sputtered. "So

Kirk and I came up with a plan this summer. It was based on one of my novels!"

How meta, I thought.

"What the hell are you talking about?" Fun demanded. "Why have you been keeping Darcy tied up down in this awful place?"

"We decided to stage a kidnapping. We were going to sequester her in the distillery until after *Grease*. Then we would 'happen' to find her. So not only would we be stars, but we'd be heroes as well. And we could pin it on Fun and Nails. That's why we burgled Miranda and Sheila's room; that's why we planted those notes and rearranged the books. It stank of Fun and Nails. Weird, kooky stuff. I mean, one's a dyslexic, and the other's a vandal; you're easy patsies. And when we found out Sheila wasn't who she said she was, when Kirk hacked into Stanton's e-mail, we sent Carli that—"

"What did I tell you, Fun?" Nails interrupted. "I told you I was a patsy. But by the way, Mary, I'm not a dyslexic. I just have a speech impediment. Childhood trauma from after my mom died and a rich Republican adopted me and changed my identity."

Fun kept quiet.

I stared at him. He tapped his foot, staring at the walls, like he wanted to cover all of them in a frenzied graffiti attack. Finally he whispered: "Nails, Miranda, Carli, and I are the good guys, and none of us is who we say we are. This is not going to look good on a college application."

Darcy straightened. "You're right," she said, in a scarily dead-on impersonation of Dean Wormer, from *Animal House.* "'The time has come to put a foot down,'" she quoted, "'and that foot is me.'"

I grinned at her. She grinned back. I raised my hands to applaud—

"Shh!" she hissed.

Footsteps were approaching. I thought of Miranda's gun. I thought of Kirk. There was only one pair of feet . . .

It was neither. It was Mr. Hines.

"What are you kids doing here at four in the morning?" he demanded.

We looked at one another. Even Mary was speechless. There was no easy or brief answer to that question.

"Sarah Ryder just called me and told me that she saw *you,* Sheila, running across campus. This is not only a major infraction of the rules; this is an offense punishable by expulsion . . ." His voice faded, his gaze locked on Darcy, the missing girl, the queen of Winchester, the rightful heir to the throne of Sandy in *Grease.*

And before he could continue, I took a cue, method-acting style, from Darcy Novak herself. I burst into tears. Honestly: waterworks.

"Mr. Hines, you don't understand!" I cried. "Kirk Bishop and Mary Fishman are responsible for all this madness! Miranda is really a private investigator and she's chasing Kirk right now, and Kirk did all this weird stuff to make everybody suspicious of one another . . ." I lost the rest of the little rant in a fit of sobs.

Mr. Hines, overwhelmed by the display of emotion, rushed to console me.

Fun, Nails, and Darcy kept hold of Mary.

I winked at Fun as I sobbed. He winked back.

Fun

Giving our official statements to the cops took a lot longer than I thought. It was basically a blur. I don't even remember my testimony. I only remember fighting to keep from smiling as I thought: *So she really CAN cry on demand. Why does she need to spend time at a boarding school to become a better actress for my dad's dumb show? She's a superstar.* Oh, and I remember watching Miranda drag Kirk past us, hands cuffed behind his back, and tossing him into the back of Lieutenant Jacobs' patrol car. He was sobbing even more uncontrollably than Carli had.

At around noon, I trudged back to my room. Nails finished before I did; he was waiting for me. He'd already begun packing. Once again, he was cranking The B-52s. It was "Rock Lobster."

"Coming clean is all for the best," he yelled over the music, then grabbed the volume knob and muted it. "After all, I don't want to live a lie my whole life. I'm gonna drop out. So what if I don't get into college?"

I shook my head at him. "You'll get into college. There's no way you won't. You're too freaking smart. You got this far on lying and cheating, didn't you?"

"That's a cheap shot."

"Why didn't you tell me, *James*?"

He let out a deep breath. "I was ashamed. Anyway, would you have believed me? That I adopted the name of the son whose family adopted *me*, but I got it backward? My real parents knew . . . his parents."

"That's it?" I asked.

Nails nodded.

"Tell me the truth!" I shouted. "Seriously, man!"

"What could I tell you? That my mom used to work for the James family, as house cleaner and babysitter? That the James family decided to take me in and raise me, because they were still grieving over their son? That they wanted to give me the education he would have gotten? I was still a screwup; they couldn't hide that. Even after they shuffled our names and school records and social security numbers, and sent me off to boarding school as their own son—always with a hefty donation as added incentive to ensure my acceptance. First Hotchkiss, then here."

I swallowed. "Jesus," I said.

"Amen," Nails agreed. "Now you know why I'm so screwed up. It's the guilt. Darcy was right; I was scary, because I was hiding something. Even Stanton makes me feel guilty! I mean . . . I love this school! Even though our principal has no principles." He brightened. "Hey, that's funny, isn't it? Principal and principles?"

"No, it isn't funny, Nails," I said dryly. "*I'm* funny. But I'm glad the Prodigal Son has returned. Reckless and redeemed."

He laughed and slapped my shoulder. "Ha! You've got it. Horace Winchester's whole point in founding this school was to try to empower the reckless. To redeem us! He wanted to give us a voice! It's a *school*, right? We're here for the teachers, not the other way around. We *need* them—but more truthfully, they need us. You know what I'm saying? Somebody should inform Stanton and Hines."

"Yeah . . ." My magnanimous mood faded, but not because

of Nails. I needed to "inform" Dad about the insanity of the past few weeks in every excruciating detail. I needed to put an end to this *Private Nights* nonsense once and for all.

"What?" Nails said.

"Nothing. I'll be right back." I sprinted out of our room down the stairs, out onto the dilapidated football field, punching in my dad's number.

"Fun!" Dad yelled in my ear. "Great to hear from you, buddy! Nice work, helping out the cops like that. Listen, *Private Nights* is doing another rewrite."

"Dad, I—"

"Just let me finish! We're going urban. The whole 'Saint Sancerre Academy' thing doesn't work if it's set in the boondocks. We want the show more cosmopolitan, more *Sex and the City.* So we're pulling you and Carli out of there."

"What?"

"You'll be flying to Washington, D.C., tomorrow afternoon and enrolling in Marshall Academy, a prep school for diplomats' and ambassadors' kids, near the vice president's mansion. I've already squared it with Winchester. Frankly, they're happy to see you go, what with all the scandal. Carli can continue to use you as an assistant while she's there, and you'll stay on to graduate. Okay? I'm sure you'll love it."

Click.

I hung up. Nice. It was wonderful to be in such control of my life.

But, hey, I really didn't have much to complain about. Why

would I want to *stay* at Winchester? Maybe I'd miss Nails, but the kid would probably be better off without me. Plus, going to school in a real city would be like being dropped smack in the middle of a huge, blank canvas: The possibilities for graffiti were limitless. And, I had to admit, hanging out with Carli was, strangely, kind of a blast. Still, when I reconnected with her later that day over fecal burgers and canned peaches in the dining hall, she seemed heartbroken at the prospect of leaving Winchester. She actually cried.

"I just got a call from your father," she sobbed. "I can't believe he'd yank us out of this school so fast, after all we've been through."

Jeez. I had no idea she liked the place so much. Especially considering the ridiculous nightmare we'd just survived. So I leaned over to give her a hug—

I caught a wink instead.

6 The punch line

Fun

There is a punch line to this whole story. Not that it's any *Portnoy's Complaint,* but still.

Stanton and Hines wanted to cancel *Grease* entirely. Nails made a big stink about how the fall musical was a big part of "The Winchester tradition"—as big a part as the students' dirty laundry or the old vineyards or the school's bad reputation—so, in typical fashion, he took a stand. He refused to allow them to cancel. Now that Darcy had been found, alive and well, he claimed the school owed it to her to let her play Sandy. He turned his blog into a virtual vigil, pleading day and night with the administration to keep the production rolling and to hold new auditions for the roles that were now vacant. He'd never gotten more of a positive response (for anything) in his entire life.

Oh, right—the punch line. Nails also tried out. He was cast as Danny.

Carli

I'm not sure if I'd call it a punch line, but I'd say it was a happy ending. (I've never read *Portnoy's Complaint.*) Neither Fun nor I knew that Nails could sing. He's got an amazing voice! Fun and I actually snuck back on campus to attend opening night.

Well, okay, Jonathan Newport flew us in and hired us a limo. It was almost like we were going to a secret prom, because we couldn't tell anyone we were there.

(We told Nails of course, and Sarah Ryder, too. She was recast as Rizzo.)

I held Fun's hand throughout the entire performance. He didn't seem to notice. Either that, or he didn't seem to care. Not sure which. Is that a punch line, too?

Turn the page for a sneak peek at Daniel Ehrenhaft's

FRIEND IS NOT A VERB

Opening Disclaimers

This is kind of a screwy story, so I'm not sure where to begin. I mean, I could tell you my name, but I've decided to change it. Seriously. I don't know what the new one will be yet, but as soon as I figure it out, I'm going to file the forms and petition the court and do whatever it takes to make it official—and if it costs money, then I'll finally get a real job. Or at least I'll play the Lotto.

Until I hit the jackpot, though, I'm stuck with Henry Birnbaum. Hen, for short.

Everyone has always called me Hen. All the major players in this screwy story have: my big sister, Sarah (who vanished under mysterious circumstances for an entire year); my girlfriend, Petra (who dumped me); my best friend, Emma (who also had that dream about going to school naked); my parents (who threatened to set fire to my dirty socks unless I "took responsibility for [my] own hygiene and put them in the hamper!"); and, lastly, Gabriel Stern, my sister's friend from college, the twenty-two-year-old fugitive who was supposed to be my bass teacher but ended up being something else entirely (a bizarro Obi-Wan to my Luke?), partly because he is such a lousy bassist himself.

The problem is, Hen doesn't fit me anymore. It's too young sounding. True, I am only sixteen, but after all the insanity of the past year, sometimes I feel like I'm a hundred. Sometimes I feel like I'm a thousand.

Anyway, my new name, whatever it is, will say something about me. Like "the guy who finally learned the freakish truth about *why* his sister disappeared." Or "He may be going through that awkward teen phase now, but watch out soon, ladies!" Except it won't be that long. It'll be short and tasty—maybe in one of those forgotten tribal languages Gabriel tried to learn while he and my sister were hiding out in the Caribbean. Those indigenous Caribbean tribes know how to do names right. (In Taino, the name "Yaya" means "the Great Spirit who Created Everything." I would say that's funky.)

Most of all, my new name will show how I've become more superstitious. How I no longer believe that there's any difference between what happens while you're asleep and while you're awake—aside from the obvious stuff, like snoring and drooling.

So enough with the opening disclaimers. There really is only one place to start: June 4, the first night of summer vacation. That was the night Petra decided she didn't want to be my girlfriend anymore—back when I blamed Gabriel and my sister for almost everything that had gone wrong in my life, even though I hardly knew why he and Sarah had disappeared in the first place.

CHAPTER ONE

Feelings

"I'm sorry, Hen. I still have feelings for you. It's just that my band needs a real bass player now. We're not a joke band anymore. Okay, sweetie?"

That was how Petra Dostoyevsky fired me.

We were standing outside the Bimbo Lounge on the Lower East Side of Manhattan. It was raining: heavy, pelting rain. Petra's hair dye was starting to run. The black drops on her cheeks were actually kind of attractive, which annoyed me. It was 9:05 P.M. Her favorite band—aside from her own—was supposed to start at 9:00. (They're called Shakes the Clown. Petra believes that they're geniuses.)

"We should still hang out," Petra added.

I nodded. I couldn't imagine any possible scenario where that might occur, but it was a nice thought.

She cast a furtive glance at the bouncer. He was bald and pale, about the size and shape of a rhinoceros. He wore a tight 2002 Britney Spears concert T-shirt under a soggy pin-striped blazer.

"Do you still want to see the show?" she asked.

"Um, no, I guess not. But—"

"Bye, Hen." She pecked me on the cheek, then turned and scurried past the bouncer—who not only held the door, but also graciously neglected to card her.

I prefer the word "fired" to "dumped," because going out with Petra was kind of like a job. Not that I'm ungrateful. Being with Petra—and being the bassist for her band, PETRA—was amazing for the month that it lasted. But it was hard work. She's pretty much a superstar—at Franklin High, anyway—so the playing field was never level. She's tall (two inches taller than me), tasteful in regard to piercings (a lone silver stud in the left nostril), and she even manages to pull off hair dye unpretentiously (jet black, but somehow not in a scary way).

Plus, I'm fairly sure she's smarter than I am.

So it was no surprise that she treated me the way a boss would. A nice boss, sure. "That's not how the bass line goes, sweetie." Or: "That T-shirt doesn't look cute on you, Hen." She even kissed me with bosslike detachment. Let's just say that there were no spontaneous moments of wild passion. She operated on a reward system. If I nailed a bass line she wrote or wore the right T-shirt, I got lucky.

The funny thing is, I never would have gone out with her in the first place if I hadn't responded to her ad in the school's online paper, *The Franklin Sentinel*. It wasn't a personal ad, either. It was an ad seeking a bassist for her band. And I guess that's the point: It's hard not to think of a relationship as a job when you have to be interviewed and pass an audition. On the other hand, there are certain moments in your life when you fall in love with a semistranger, instantly and deliriously. For me, that moment was when I read that ad.

Day 5,882 of a life that never seems to end . . .

"It would be an unsound fancy and self-contradictory to expect that things which have never yet been done can be done except by means which have never yet been tried."

—Sir Francis Bacon

Dearest Franklinites,

You'll notice a quote above this week's post. I have no idea what the quote means. Is that why I got a D on my last philosophy quiz? Maybe.

The point of this post: I won't be allowed to blog for a while, owing to poor grades, lack of focus, and an "attitude problem." So I'm starting a band. I already have a drummer lined up, and I am the guitarist/front woman/vixen. (There, I said it.) Now I need a bassist. Do any of you play bass? If so, please hit me back at: petrad@franklin.edu . . . Auditions start tomorrow at 3:30 at Sonic Rehearsal Studios!

xoxo Petra

As far as the audition went:

I was the only one who showed up. Nobody else had

bothered, probably because they assumed Petra was joking.

When I arrived at Sonic Rehearsal Studios after a perfunctory email exchange, I felt like the victim of a prank. The "Studios" consisted of a single room at the back of a bodega. It wasn't much bigger than a broom closet. It *smelled* like a broom closet, dank and musty.

Petra stood alone amid the decrepit amplifiers and drums in a black sweater, miniskirt, leggings, and boots.

"Hi," I said, nervously clutching my bass case.

"Thanks for coming. Hen, isn't it?" Her dark eyes brightened. "Wait! You're that guy whose sister disappeared, right?"

"Yup, that's me," I said. "The guy whose sister disappeared."

"Oh, my God—" She clasped a hand over her mouth. "Sorry, that was so rude."

"Don't worry about it."

She stared down at her boots, then blinked shyly at me. "Well, let me make it up to you," she said. "Play me a song. I promise I'll be more objective than usual."

I glanced around. "Shouldn't we wait for your drummer?

"He's not coming," she said. "He was sort of bummed out. I mean, since you're the only one who answered the ad."

"Oh," I said.

Looking back now, I realize that this conversation may have marked the high point of our relationship. I plugged in and plucked out four measures of Queen's "Another One Bites the Dust." (If I were a pianist, this would be like auditioning with "Chopsticks.") Petra applauded wildly after my pathetic performance, then jumped forward and kissed me on the lips—

quickly and naturally, as if we'd known each other for years. She told me I was in the band.

I'd never felt as wonderful, not even when we made out in her bedroom two days later and officially became a couple for the next month. During that one moment, I was in paradise.

Back to the night she fired me:

"On second thought, I do *want to see the show,"* I imagined telling her, seconds into my brand-new role as her ex-boyfriend. What if I'd pretended to be cheerfully clueless? *"You said we should still hang out, right? Let's go!"* That would have been funny. On the other hand, she probably wouldn't have appreciated the joke.

So, all right, one thing that did bug me about Petra: She was funnier in writing than she was in person. A lot of times, even in normal conversation, she sounded as if she were pitching a TV commercial to a bunch of ad execs. She insisted that every recent pop-culture phenomenon was nothing more than a recycled bit of something brilliant in the past.

Maybe that's why I wasn't all that upset about being fired by Petra outside the Bimbo Lounge. But *that* was upsetting, the fact that nothing could upset me—not even this beautiful girl who had ditched me in the rain. At the time, I chalked it up to the old bully's rule of the playground: Punch an arm long enough and eventually that arm goes numb. Lord knows that my proverbial arm had been beaten senseless. Try to see it from my perspective. Or better yet, try to see it from *your* perspective: Here's this loser, and his sister has been missing for a year; his parents are slowly losing their minds; his grades have long since circled the drain; last night he forgot yet again to put his socks in the hamper . . . and now his girlfriend has abandoned him.

Does that sound self-pitying?

Good. I think I'm entitled to a little self-pity now and then.

There was an upside, though. Standing on that grim sidewalk—fired, and alone—I had six simultaneous epiphanies:

1. Petra is very shallow and self-obsessed. I'm better off without her.
2. Okay, that's a big lie. Petra is hot and smart and funny (in writing), and even if she's annoying sometimes, nobody is better off without a girl like that.
3. The only reason Petra went out with me was because she needed a bass player for PETRA.
4. PETRA was never a joke band, and I'm a terrible bass player . . . and, wait, there goes George Monroe into the club. Hmm. George shreds on bass, and he's also better looking than I am, and he's actually a really nice guy—and now I bet he's stealing my job and my girlfriend.
5. I want to be angry with George for this if it's true, but I'm not, and I'm not sure why (though it probably comes back to the old rule of the playground).
6. In spite of her shallow self-obsession, Petra is honest. She fired me because she needs a replacement, and I'm sure it's George—I mean, come on; what are the chances that he just showed up here?—and he can actually get into a Lower East Side club, whereas I probably can't.

From inside, I heard the faint strains of Shakes the Clown's opener, a modified cover of the seventies soft-rock classic: "Feelings . . . nothing more than feelings . . ."

There wasn't much point in hanging around. Plus, I needed to make the Emma call.

Whenever I suffer, whenever I rejoice, whenever those occasions arise when I think I might be close to slipping closer to the abyss of insanity, I make a point to talk it all through with my next-door neighbor Emma Wood. Skinny, neurotic, ratty haired, reclusive Emma Wood—she is and always has been the only person who can convince me that I am, in fact, still sane. Or at least sane in comparison to her.

More than my next-door neighbor, Emma Wood has been my sort-of sister for the past decade. She assumed that role ever since my *real* sister babysat the two of us at Emma's house after Emma moved in with her quiet mom and nut-job dad.

I hunched over my cell phone and dialed.

"Wow, that's so weird!" she answered.

"What is?"

"I was just going to call you," she said. "I now have proof that there is no God. The band Journey still exists. What label would carry them? It was bad enough when Mom told me that 'Lovin', Touchin', Squeezin'' was 'their' song. You know how much the wedding video traumatized me. But now they're actually going to pay to see the so-called reunited Journey in concert. Anyway, Dad said I could bring you, and I was wondering if you wanted to go. I mean, for comic value—"

"Emma?" I interrupted. My teeth chattered. I was wet and miserable.

"Yeah, I know. You don't remember who Journey is. I'll give you a hint. Picture my mom, circa 1983. Then start singing, 'Just a small town girl—'"

"No. She finally did it. Petra broke up with me. Then she kicked me out of her band. In that order."

"Hen, you can't get too upset about this," she warned. "Remember that *Simpsons* episode, when Lisa said that the Chinese have the same word for both crisis and opportunity? This is a classic case of 'crisi-tunity'! Make the most of it."

"Seriously, Emma, I thought you liked Petra."

"The person or the band?" She snorted. "Listen, Hen, I say a lot of stuff. I once said that her band might have a shot at making it big. But I didn't say the stuff you need to hear. Like how Petra always sneaks a peek at herself in any reflective surface."

"That's what I need to hear?" I asked.

"No, but she's raised self-obsession to an art form. And you had something she wanted."

I almost laughed. "What's that?"

"You have this edgy mystique," Emma said.

Then I did laugh. For a second, I forgot about the rain. I even forgot about how the rain might short-circuit my cell phone and electrocute me. "You want to run that by me again?"

"You're the guy whose sister disappeared, remember? Petra said it herself."

"Yeah, I remember," I said.

"You were even on the news."

Yes, Emma, I remember, I grumbled silently.

And what a fifteen minutes of fame it was. About a week before school started in the fall, a twentysomething blond reporter—a real go-getter, at least judging from the amount of hair product and makeup she wore—showed up at our door with her trusty bearded cameraman sidekick. They arrived on the heels of the police's third and final visit, basically to ask the same question: Why would a smart, attractive, white (apparently even with our black president, America isn't still *quite* "post-racial") twenty-two-year-old Ivy League grad vanish with four friends without any explanation? The response Mom and Dad gave to the reporter and her cameraman—which was the same response they'd given to the cops— was: "We have no idea. Yes, we are a close family. No, she doesn't have any skeletons in her closet. Neither do we. Yes, we are worried and shocked. . . ."

The twisted part? I knew better. Mom and Dad *did* know why Sarah had run away, and moreover, why she was wanted by law enforcement. And the *truly* criminal part? They refused to tell me. So did the cops, but for a different and much more understandable reason: They couldn't jeopardize an ongoing investigation.

Anyway, the reporter and the cameraman wouldn't take the hint to leave. And just at the very moment Mom and Dad started screaming at "Blondie and the Beard" to "get the hell off our stoop!!!" (Mom actually addressed them in the third person as such), I strolled into camera range. There was a choice shot of me, with my jaw hanging open, looking like a lobotomy patient. It made both the six and eleven o'clock broadcasts.

Emma sighed on the other end. "Listen, Hen, this is going to sound harsh, but Petra never saw you for who you are. To her, you're just this guy with a runaway sister—so even though you don't realize it yourself, you do have this semicriminal aura, which is always great for a band. Plus, on a more practical level, you have a really kick-ass bass rig—"

"Petra did say she had feelings for me," I interrupted.

"Any dump*er* says that she still has 'feelings' for the dump*ee*, Hen," Emma groaned. "It's a perennial. It's in a thousand cheesy songs. Speaking of which: What about this Journey concert?"

"Um . . . I'll let you know," I said. "Bye, Emma." I closed the cell phone and shoved it back into my damp pocket.

Maybe Emma was right. Maybe the only reason Petra had gone out with me was because I was the "guy whose sister disappeared," and I had a kick-ass bass rig. The silly irony is that the only reason my parents bought me such a rig was because they felt guilty about having spent most of last year obsessing over Sarah and keeping me in the dark about why she was gone.

As if it even merits a mention, their extravagant expenditure did not make up for their incomprehensible behavior or for the fact that I have very little musical talent.

But that's not even the best part.

After a long, lonely subway ride back to Brooklyn (the train smelled), I arrived to find a note dangling precariously from a piece of tape on the front door of the Birnbaum family brownstone.

Hen,

Guess what? Sarah came home! ☜

Can you believe it? She made us swear not to tell anyone she's here. We're at the airport, picking her up. We'll be back at about 11:30 depending on traffic.

Love you,

Mom

PS: There's some leftover Chinese in the fridge. We got you vegetable lo mein. But try not to finish it. Dad wants some.

PPS: Try to clean your room a little, too, before we get home, okay? It would be nice for Sarah.

JUST SO YOU KNOW, THIS BOOK IS ABOUT HOW MY LIFE WENT **COMPLETELY BERSERK.**

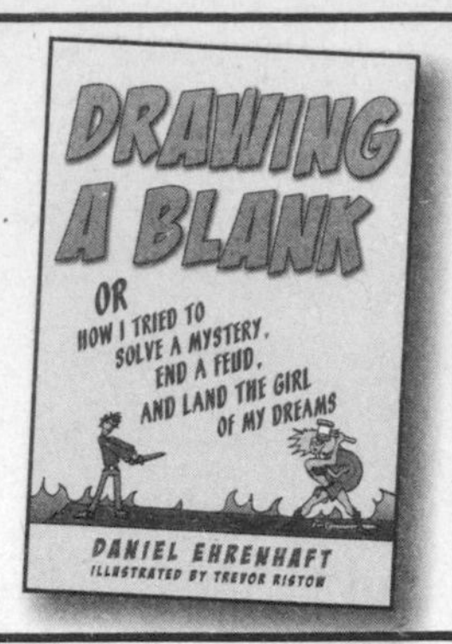

One day I'm snug in my comic book drawing, loner existence, and the next I'm tramping through the wilderness looking for my dad. Who's been kidnapped.

Now my only company is a wannabe cop who just might be my superhero dream girl. And if I don't deliver some kind of mysterious "proof" to his kidnappers, my dad is toast. I've got some issues, but I don't really want to see him burned to a crisp.